CW00926168

Motive for murder

A sharp and startling green, like emeralds viewed through sea water, only the vagrant's eyes are visible.

A brick lies near his head, several strands of long grey hair adhering to it. But the stab wounds to his abdomen are really the cause of death.

DCI Ian Roper is mystified. The six pounds in the tramp's pocket seem to rule out one motive; another down-and-out would surely have taken both the cash and the bottle of Bells which lies next to the body. But why bash his skull in when he was already dead? Heat of the moment? Drugs? Self-defence? Blackmail?

As the Rickenham Green police HQ starts to hum with the nervous activity which heralds a major murder investigation, across town a young girl – a heroin addict – discharges herself secretly from the local hospital; a block of flats behind the Station Arms is burgled; an attempted suicide is foiled; and the devious machinations of a small-time pimp are exposed. All are linked to a complex and baffling homicide which threatens the social fabric of a small town and ends with a startling – and literary – revelation.

In her third novel Janie Bolitho again displays her formidable talents for plotting and characterisation in a whodunnit of extraordinary tension and pace.

Also by Janie Bolitho

Kindness can kill (1993)
Ripe for revenge (1994)

MOTIVE FOR MURDER

Janie Bolitho

Constable · London

First published in Great Britain 1994
by Constable & Company Ltd
3 The Lanchesters, 162 Fulham Palace Road
London W6 9ER
Copyright © 1994 by Janie Bolitho
The right of Janie Bolitho to be
identified as the author of this work
has been asserted by her in accordance
with the Copyright, Designs and Patents Act 1988
ISBN 0 09 473560 3
Set in Linotron Palatino 11 pt by
CentraCet Limited, Cambridge
Printed and bound in Great Britain by
Hartnolls Limited, Bodmin, Cornwall

A CIP catalogue record for this book
is available from the British Library

For Julian and Emma

1

The tramp lived at the far end of the town, the dross end, where more buildings stood derelict than in use.

The railway station, now a branch line, once boasted a thriving goods depot and before the surrounding warehouses had become obsolete there were rows of well-kept terraced houses where railway staff and their families lived. The pubs had done good business and the corner shops gave credit safe in the knowledge that accounts would be settled each week.

Then Rickenham Green was a true market town with animals and farm vehicles cluttering up the roads twice a week. The present market consisted of no more than a handful of stalls at the top of the High Street which sold overpriced bedding plants and gaudy T-shirts which stretched in the wash.

All that was left now in the station area were run-down properties and the Station Arms, a barn of a bar rarely used and with mould in the corners of the bedrooms once used by travelling salesmen. And hoardings. They were everywhere. The only purpose they seemed to serve was to provide a surface for fly-posters to display their advertisements. There was nothing behind the wooden boards that needed protection, unless piles of rubble half hidden in the long grass counted.

The residents of the high-rise flats adjacent had resourcefully prised loose a couple of planks and used the waste ground to dispose of their larger pieces of rubbish, saving themselves a trip to the dump and thereby providing the tramps, the homeless and the vagrants with enough raw material to set up home. They lived there undisturbed. Clear them out and they would only find somewhere else. One or two harboured the idea of being housed, others were happy as they were. Some were past caring.

The tramp was foul and filthy. The clothes on his unwashed body were held together by sweat and dirt and string and would disintegrate if they were removed. Layer upon layer of them, winter and summer. He smelled of every excretion that was human and some that seemed not to be.

His hair was thin and grey and straggled lankly to his shoulders, but his beard was luxuriant.

Only his eyes were visible. They were green, a sharp and startling colour, like emeralds viewed through sea water. Hundreds of lines fanned out around them ingrained with dirt, giving the appearance of a perpetual smile. He lived by his wits, and they were far sharper than would be credited to him at first sight.

Monday night. He was in the town centre, the modern bit where the new Town Hall stood and the glass and concrete office blocks had sprung up to replace small businesses. Half the windows were lit, the pattern random. He was well away from his home territory; here the best pickings were to be had. He had learned that long ago. Businessmen and office girls dropped half-eaten rolls and sandwiches into waste bins, mindless of the cost. But here, too, if he hung around until the offices closed for the night, he had been known to make as much as five pounds in one hit.

The tramp knew his business. These people had homes, wives, meals waiting. It was easier for them to hand him a few coins rather than have him pestering them, delaying their return home. He no longer bothered to go near the supermarket. Mothers with pushchairs and toddlers and shopping were too harassed, too pre-occupied and too short of cash themselves to fumble in their handbags for their purses. And some of the older ones looked through him as if he did not exist. He was used to it, hardened to it, and it no longer bothered him.

The weather was on the turn. September had been hot, the whole summer had been unusually hot, but now there was a nip in the air and last night, behind the hoardings, they'd made a fire. In a week or two they would build it high and blazing, he and Tommy and Josie and Mad Dora and Bill, who insisted he'd once been somebody and was consequently named 'Sir William'. They would sit around the fire, their fronts warm, their backs frozen, firelight dancing over their lived-in faces, and they would talk, or be silent, except for Mad Dora who was never sient, even in sleep. And drink, if they were lucky, drink themselves into oblivion if they could because that way the long, cold nights passed more quickly.

Nearly all the office lights were extinguished. He had already made a bob or two. It was dusk, almost dark, and the starlings twittered noisily in the tall saplings planted in equally spaced gaps in the paving stones. A man appeared, one of the last to leave. The tramp held out his hand. 'Can you spare a few coppers for a cup of tea?'

The man carried a raincoat over his arm and a briefcase in his hand. With his spare hand he flipped back the front of his jacket with practised ease and reached deep into his trouser pocket. His mouth was set in a grim line, his forehead creased with anxiety. He was desperately troubled; his actions were automatic.

'Here,' the man said, 'take this.'

The tramp looked at the fifty-pence piece in his hand.

It was his lucky day, it took the takings to over six pounds. He glanced up to say thank you and in that split second recognised the man.

The emerald eyes narrowed as he spoke.

The man in the suit blanched when he heard what the tramp said. 'I, er . . .' The brain behind the ashen face worked overtime as he tried to decide what to do.

A brief conversation followed. The emerald eyes widened, the expression incalculable. The tramp walked towards the nearest off-licence that would allow him through its door. In his hand was a ten-pound note. Not wishing anyone to oberve that he was in possession of that kind of money, he screwed it into a ball and clutched it tightly. And there was more to come.

The following Monday he waited again outside the offices. This time he walked away with a wide grin and twenty pounds. How odd, he thought as he shuffled along to the same off-licence, that life should choose this particular time to be good to him. It did not cross his mind that it was even more odd to believe it had at all.

As he left the pedestrianised area his head was full of the idea of a regular income. The money would not be used for material things – except maybe a pair of boots – but spent on whisky. Ten-year-old malt did not interest him, Bell's was his tipple. He might even share some of his luck with the others, Sir William for certain, for Sir William, he knew, *had* been someone. His own life had never amounted to much: odd jobs here and there. He worked hard at them but they were always temporary. There was some streak in him which prevented permanence; the urge to move on always overcame him. He had been in Rickenham long enough but there was no thought of leaving now, not until his source had run out, which, he knew, in the end it would, one way or another.

He did not expect it to be so soon.

The bottle of Bell's in its blue tissue wrapping was safely in the deep pocket of his coat. He patted it from time to time, taking comfort in its presence.

Back behind the hoardings he skirted the edge, avoiding Mad Dora and Tommy. In the darkness he knew he could not be seen. He stumbled over broken masonry and made for the far side where the dual carriageway ran parallel to the fence. He sat and waited, unperturbed by the cold, damp air, warm enough for the moment in his many layers. He uncapped the bottle and tipped it to his lips, welcoming the initial burning as the liquid went down his throat. 'Not too fast,' he told himself, 'make it last.'

By nine he was drowsy, his head nodding on to his chest as he sat propped against the boards. The neck of the bottle was between his thumb and middle finger. It was only half empty.

He did not hear the footsteps when they came. He looked up, his expression of expectancy changing to one of confusion. He looked at the bottle. No, he had not drunk enough to be hallucinating. He'd had a few swigs then gone for a walk. There was something he'd needed to do but it had gone wrong. However, what he was waiting for would compensate. But this was not the man he was waiting for. The one standing over him was menacing. He did not understand it.

'What do you want?'

He did not hear the answer, if there was one. Instead he felt a hard, pushing sensation quickly followed by a searing pain. He tried to stand but couldn't. The second time it happened he was only half conscious. In the seconds before he died he did not see his whole life flashing before him; all he was aware of was a liquid warmth. It was almost pleasant.

The footsteps retreated as silently as they had approached. The remains of the Bell's whisky trickled slowly out of the bottle as it lay on its side where he had dropped it.

He remained slumped against the fence, his eyes half open, glittering, as if he was doing no more than contemplating an irritating problem.

His second visitor came later.

2

Detective Chief Inspector Roper was experiencing feelings which were, if not entirely new, certainly unusual. Satisfaction and a touch of smugness. He studied the figures for his Division. Serious crime was down, for the moment, petty criminals were being apprehended, for the moment, and the paperwork in the right-hand basket on his desk stood only an inch above the rim. It wouldn't last, he knew that, but, he told himself, he would enjoy it. For the moment. He continued to wade through his in-tray and, in this contented frame of mind, almost, but not quite, began to feel at home in his office. There was too much chrome and glass for his taste and his polished wooden desk remained unchipped and unsullied by the rings of coffee mugs.

He glanced at a memo concerning the setting up of the Help Desk, an innovation which had already been in operation for months and to which they were already accustomed. Only when he read the heading did he feel a twinge of regret. Or was it shame? Perhaps a bit of both. The slip of paper, neatly set out by a typist, had his own name at the top left and that of Superintendent Ross on the right. But Ross was gone and his departure had been partly Ian's doing. That was the cause of his regret: he had helped to end the man's career. But Ross was bent. Not totally, but enough to turn a blind eye where his brother was concerned, and that was the reason for Ian Roper's shame. The knowledge that there were bad apples rankled, especially when most of them were trying so hard to create a better public image. Ian did not know how many men and women made up the whole of the police force but the number was so great it was impossible for there not to be corruption here and there. He screwed up the outdated memo and threw it in the direction of the full waste bin where it joined the overflow on the floor. Not even this uncomfortable memory disturbed his equilibrium for long. Ross had been replaced by Superintendent Thorne, a Brummie, whose accent was often unsuccessfully mimicked: a good man who had already earned the respect his position warranted.

Not only were things – temporarily – quiet at work; he had spent the weekend at home, not once interrupted by the telephone, an unusual occurrence in recent years.

Yesterday he had arrived at work with a groundless sense of foreboding but nothing dreadful had happened in his absence. He returned home at six, his wife, Moira, poured him a drink and he sat down to Lancashire hot-pot. For three whole days he had lived as millions of others. Now, at nearly eleven o'clock on Tuesday morning, he started to feel relaxed. The clear-up rate was improving, the paperwork was decreasing. Someone had once told him that if the contents of an in-tray were left long enough they would become obsolete and you could bin the lot.

DCI Ian Roper ran a hand through his dark hair, still thick at the back and on top but sparser, now, at the temples. He stretched in his chair, arms behind his head, then pressed a button on his intercom. His face was strong, the chin square, but what could have been seen as a stern expression was softened by the light hazel eyes which crinkled at the corners when he smiled – which he did now, knowing there was absolutely no further excuse for procrastination. He asked a secretary to come in. He really must get on with some correspondence. He asked for a particular girl by name. If or when she left he would have no alternative but to switch to a dictating machine. She was one of the few with short-hand skills.

Ian's office was on the first floor of the Rickenham Green headquarters. It was well over two years now since the move but everything still had a newness about it. Old HQ was still spoken of with fondness, its inconvenient location since the expansion of the town, its ineffective heating system and the greenhouse effect in summer all soon forgotten.

His office door was ajar; the tan wood veneer held his name-plate screwed to it a few millimetres off centre, a constant source of irritation he kept meaning to remedy. Staff passed in ones and twos, no one in any hurry. There were no raised voices, no sense of urgency. The baking heat of August, when crime escalated, was behind them and there were eight weeks before the pre-Christmas rush when criminal activity hotted up again.

'Sir?'

He looked up, expecting his secretary. Detective Sergeant Markham pushed the door a little wider. In his hand was a sheet of paper.

'Yes?'

'It's just come in. A local beat bobby called it.'

Ian took the paper. It did not tell him much but what it did say was enough to get the adrenalin surging through him. The unnatural calm of the last couple of days was already a thing of the past. He was up and running again. He opened his mouth, but the question he was about to ask became superfluous as Markham said, 'The wheels are in motion, sir. Doc Harris is the only one I can't get hold of. He's been called to an emergency.'

Ian glanced at his watch. 'Get his assistant.'

'I've already done that.'

The Chief struggled to keep the surprise from his face. DS Markham was an excellent thief-taker. Accepted, his methods were sometimes a little unorthodox, but he was not renowned for initiative when it came to police procedure. Given the choice he would have done away with it altogether. His initiative was kept for the streets where he was happiest. However, today he seemed to have used some.

'Shall I drive you, sir?'

'You might as well.' Ian cancelled his request for a secretary, picked up his lightweight raincoat and followed Markham down the corridor.

They walked down the single flight of concrete steps, Markham slightly ahead, always impatient to be doing something. He was a little over six foot, proud of his physique and, at thirty-six, the fitness he had managed to maintain. His hair, cropped short, added to the menace of his smile.

At the foot of the stairs, to the left, was a large, open-plan area which held several desks, each with its own telephone and computer. It housed the detectives and was known as the general office. As elsewhere in the station, it was quiet. One or two were on annual leave; the few that were in were catching up on reports and paperwork.

'Have they all been informed?' the Chief asked.

'Yes. Except DS Swan.'

Detective Sergeant Barry Swan chose that moment to saunter in through the door on the far side of the general office. The Chief beckoned him over.

'Morning, sir. Something come up?' Ian and Barry had been a team for a long time. In private they used each other's first names; in front of other staff they were more formal, although it was not strictly necessary.

'A tramp? But why? We're certain it is murder?' Barry thought it more likely the man had taken a fall after too many drinks or got into a fight with one of his colleagues.

'It's murder.'

'Need me along?'

'Not yet. Markham's set it up.'

Barry raised a surprised eyebrow and the Chief grinned back sardonically. Markham did not see. He was already heading out of the swing doors in the main entrance, car keys swinging on his index finger.

He pulled out of the car-park and turned left, then he reached under the dashboard for the magnetised siren which could be clamped to the roof of an unmarked car.

'I don't think so, Markham. It's a little late for that, don't you think? And I suggest, unless you want us to become corpses too, you slow down a fraction.'

Markham did so, his face expressionless. The Chief was aware of his driving habits. It was one of the reasons he had hesitated over his promotion. Anyone who drove at high speed, or used the siren when not necessary, was open to question. But he had sailed through driver training after his two compulsory years with the force and followed it up with the advanced course. Students with over-confident or aggressive attitudes were usually weeded out very quickly, yet Markham had lasted the course, displaying neither of these disadvantages. And, to be fair, the Chief was used to Barry Swan, who despite his flash image, kept well within the speed limit. At least he did when the Chief was in the car.

The flow of traffic through the town centre was not heavy at that time of day and they were soon approaching the new part, unaware that the dead man had spent the early part of the previous evening just to the left of where they were stopped at a pedestrian crossing. One of the young trees in the paved square had already been snapped in half and a soft drink can floated in the

15

ornamental pond beneath the fountain. 'New', the Chief decided, reminded of his own office, 'does not necessarily mean better.'

They waited at red lights, Markham wisely slowing down on amber. The commercial area was to the left; on the right were several flourishing shops patronised by the office workers. There was a shoe repair shop, a baker's which also provided filled rolls and sandwiches, a dry cleaner and a florist which stayed open until seven thirty, handy for men returning late to their wives. It was all very chic but lacked the character and friendliness of the older parts of town. Unfortunately building societies and estate agents now lined the High Street and at the top of it two supermarkets vied for trade, incongruous beside St Luke's church and its lich-gate, both of which had remained unchanged for several hundred years.

The road they were in had quietened down lately. No longer did the rumble of bulldozers and clatter of pneumatic drills rend the air. Raw patches of earth exposed by the developers had already acquired a covering of grass and the shrubs planted earlier in the year were filmed with diesel fumes and dust.

The lights changed to green but Markham waited while an ambulance, siren blaring, overtook them. It was on its way to another disaster, where, hopefully, unlike their own destination, it would not be too late.

The next intersection, also with its own set of traffic lights, was the end of anything resembling the community life of Rickenham Green in its smaller, more rural days. Here was waste ground where houses once stood. Some bits were boarded up, others left open. Children from the flats gathered there to play or fight and dogs roamed freely, fouling the overgrown grass and rank weeds.

The Station Arms carried on business but it was badly

run down, the landlady aware that it, too, was ear-marked for development.

Parked on the left and causing a hold-up in the traffic was a patrol car, its blue light silent, but swirling as a warning to oncoming vehicles. In front of it were two unmarked cars, which the Chief recognised as coming from the police pool, and a small van. Markham pulled into the space in front of the van.

A uniformed man, PC Walters, stood guard at the unofficial entrance to the area behind the hoardings. Chief Inspector Roper introduced himself and his companion.

'You called this one, I believe? Did you discover the body yourself?'

'No, sir. It was another vagrant. He approached me in the street, just there, sir.' Walters pointed. 'I was doing my usual rounds and he came up to me and said, "You'd better take a look in there." Then he disappeared.'

'Disappeared? Didn't you question him first, or ask him to accompany you?'

Walters' face reddened. 'No, I'm sorry, sir, but I didn't think I was going to find a body.'

'Just what did you think?'

'I . . . I don't really know, sir. I would've questioned him otherwise.'

His excuse was ignored for what it was. 'The man said nothing else?'

'No, sir.'

'Do you know anything about him?' Men like Walters infuriated him – unambitious, uncaring and content to pick up their wage packets while they waited for retire-ment whilst doing as little as possible. They were also the ones who tended to believe they knew their own patch and what was going on in it better than anyone. Usually they were wrong.

'Who, sir? The deceased, or the man who alerted me?'

17

'Either.'

'I know most of them by sight and some by their nicknames. The one who told me, I believe he's the one they call Sir William.'

'You believe, do you? God help me. Either you know or you don't.' Getting information out of Walters was worse than interrogating a suspect. They were supposed to be on the same side.

'I'm pretty certain I'm right.'

'Okay. How many of them use this place?'

'About five or six. Never more than that. They don't let newcomers in.'

'And where would they have been while their mate was getting himself killed?'

'I don't know. They sleep here but you hardly ever see them around during the day.'

It seemed that Walters was assuming the man was killed that morning, and that might just be because he thought Sir William had done it, which made the case against him worse. Even more reason to detain him.

'Carry on with what you're doing for the time being. Come on,' he said, turning to Markham who was standing, hands in pockets, kicking bits of gravel into the road.

They ducked through the gap and saw, in the distance, two uniformed men, the unmistakable stooped figure of John Cotton, head of Scene-of-Crime, and one or two others, presumably the plan maker and photographer. Another man, wielding a video camera on his shoulder, was filming the body and surrounding area before anything was touched. The Chief nodded his approval. It was unusual for so many of the team to be able to arrive so expediently. Things must be quiet everywhere.

John Cotton stepped carefully away from the remains of what had once been a living person. 'Bad enough now. We can thank our lucky stars putrefaction hasn't set in as well.' John Cotton lit a cigarette, knowing it was forbidden at the scene, but he was all right smoking here – they were out of doors and he now stood sufficiently far away for it not to interfere with any evidence.

'Ian, Markham,' he said belatedly by way of greeting. 'Looks like nothing's been touched. Peregrine Danvers is here.' He lowered his head and looked over the top of his glasses in a familiar gesture of secret mirth. 'He's certified him dead and he's waiting until I've done my stuff before he examines him properly. I've already found a brick, near his head. There were several strands of long, grey hair adhering to it. The side of his skull's been bashed in, doesn't need a medic to see that, but there's hardly any blood. I've bagged the brick. Who's on exhibits?'

'I haven't decided yet.'

'It was too far away for him to have fallen on it.' John Cotton was off on his own trail of thought.

'What?'

'Sorry. The brick, over three feet away, the trajectory isn't right. More likely someone dropped it after hitting him. Only assuming the hairs match, that is. Ah, here come the screens.'

They were placed around the body to protect the sensitivity of the curious and the morbid, although there was no evidence of either. Apart from the victim and his attending entourage, the waste ground was deserted. PC Walters could hopefully be trusted to keep people away – he had managed so far to keep an accurate record of team members and the time they arrived. It would not do for a truant child to slip in unobserved.

John Cotton methodically went over the ground immediately surrounding the body, sighing when he saw how little there was to go on. Doc Harris's assistant waited patiently. He was a lot younger than his superior, less phlegmatic, and lacked his sense of humour. He

19

was also new to the job. Within the makeshift privacy of the screens he was at last able to make his examination. He put the time of death at between ten to fifteen hours previously, thus nullifying PC Walters' theory. Peregrine Danvers' manner of speech was formal and precise. He came over as rather bumptious. The Chief made allowances, knowing that, given time, he would loosen up. He would need to when he found out how much humour his name aroused.

The arrival of the Home Office pathologist took them by surprise. They were few and far between and often had long distances to cover. Harry Ford lived thirty-five miles away, closer than many in other areas, but his arrival was still considered prompt. 'Hello, Ian,' he said. 'Lucky for you I was already out. Got the call on the car phone. I hate the damn things but it saved going home. Have Forensics finished yet?'

'Almost, I think.'

'Five minutes, no more,' John Cotton informed them.

Ian made small talk with Harry, asking after his first grandchild, but he was impatient to get started on the case. Markham was occupied making notes of any verbal information which might speed things up.

'Ah, they've finished. It's all yours, Harry.'

Harry Ford approached the body using the designated route. He examined the victim's neck and face, rolled back his eyelids and, having checked that it was in order to move the body, turned it on its back. He stood up. 'It looks as if stab wounds to the abdomen are the likely cause of death.'

'But . . . John?' When the Chief had arrived the body was lying face down, the legs bent at an angle, the head wound clearly visible. Only now could the bloodstained clothing be seen.

'Didn't say he was *killed* with the brick, Ian. I only said

20

he was probably hit with it. After he was dead. Hence so little blood.'

'Jesus!'

'Interesting,' John Cotton said. 'I don't mean to tread on your toes, you're the detective, but there's over six pounds in his pocket. Doesn't look like the motive was robbery. And if my guess is right, he dropped this as he fell.' In a clear plastic bag was an empty whisky bottle, placed there so as not to destroy fingerprints or traces of saliva. 'The angle's right and there's a damp patch underneath where it lay, still smells of alcohol. And this', he added appreciatively, 'is what I like a drop of myself.'

Ian was mystified. Another vagrant would surely have taken both the money and the booze, unless he or she had panicked. But why bash his skull in when he was already dead? It was a question they would all ask many times in the days to come.

He needed to think, to picture what might have happened. He strolled away from the group, still busy inside and outside the screens, and took in his surroundings carefully. He could no longer recall what once stood on the spot but it was hardly relevant. He was used to the sight of death but he still hated having to face it, never knowing what to expect, yet subconsciously prepared for the worst. Strange, he reflected as he headed for the opposite side, in the open air death did not seem so awful, at least, not to him. Perhaps it was because when a victim's personal domain was violated as well it became a double degradation.

He came across a pile of boxes and some sheets of rusty corrugated iron which had been erected to form a very basic shelter. Beneath this were several extremely unhygienic mattresses and the remains of a fire, the ashes cold. He turned his back on the pitiful domestic scene and stared across the expanse of rubble and weeds. Looking at the screens he decided it would have been impossible to discern anything from that distance at night. Peregrine Danvers placed the time of death as between 9 p.m. last night and 2 a.m. this morning. If it was during the later hours the occupants would probably have been asleep. The time margin would be narrowed down after further tests, but even if the dead man's companions had been awake it was unlikely they had seen anything beyond the flames.

'Hello,' he shouted experimentally. His voice was whipped away by the wind. He shouted again, louder this time. No one turned round. It was likely, then, that no cries were heard either. If there had been any. The traffic was a constant drone, lighter at night, but always there, and the weather last night was the same as now, damp and chilly with a westerly breeze.

He walked back to where the work was taking place and issued instructions that he wanted the whole area searched for the murder weapon which was believed to be a medium-sized knife, the sort that could be found in most kitchens, then he asked Markham to drive him back. He did so, very sedately. The Chief wondered if he was being silently sarcastic.

'What do you make of it?'

Markham shook his head. 'If it was one of his chums, how come he's still in funds? I'll ask around, see if I can come up with anything.'

'Good.' The Chief knew that Markham had an excellent network of informers, more than any of the others, including himself. Markham mixed in those circles and was trusted. He never made deals unless he could keep to them. If anyone on the streets knew anything, Markham would be the one to find out.

'Right,' the Chief said when everyone was assembled for a briefing, 'this is the area we're concentrating on.'

He indicated a large-scale map on the wall. The pinboard next to it, used for putting up additional information, was empty. They had no additional information, not even a name.

'I want everyone of no fixed abode interviewed, especially those that slept down there with our man. I want to know where they were, who they were with, and I want their names. Their real names. More important, I want the victim's name. You can keep to your usual pairs.' Except Markham, of course, who preferred to work alone, his preference a great relief to his fellow officers who never knew how to take him. 'Markham, you concentrate on the off-licences, etc. There's no identifying sticker on the bottle, could've been a supermarket, but there won't have been too many with his description purchasing the stuff over the past day or so. Someone'll remember. Find out how he paid for it. I can't imagine he used a credit card, even a stolen one – it would have been queried at the time. But check anyway. The rest of you, out on the streets. DC Campbell, you can get on to the respective duty sergeants – I want the beat men interviewed. They're closest to these people. And I want the man known as Sir William found quickly. One more thing. I do not want this matter treated lightly. Whatever this man's station was in life, it is still a murder inquiry.'

He returned to his office cursing PC Walters, who should have been able to provide more information.

His stomach rumbled with hunger; his appetite always increased with his workload. Keeping the extra pounds at bay was a constant struggle but Moira did her best to encourage him. Now, whilst the procedural wheels were being set in motion, was the time to get something to eat. He went back down to the ground floor, past the back of the reception area, and descended a further flight of steps to the basement level. The aroma, a mixture of chips and bacon and coffee, assailed him as he entered the canteen, causing his mouth to water. With a reflexive action, he slid his thumb between the belt of his trousers and his shirt. There was room enough to do so. Just. Feeling virtuously abstemious he gave the chips a miss.

'Cottage pie and veg, please, love.' The girl behind the counter dolloped the mince and potato on to a plate and added some soggy carrot rings before dipping the slotted spoon into the tray of lukewarm, tinned peas. Under the lamps keeping it warm, the food had probably lost most of its nutritional value but it was fuel to keep him going until whatever time he could get away.

He chose one of the empty tables – there were only a few people sipping tea or coffee now, and by the time he had eaten he was the only one present. He had still reached no conclusions when he returned his tray of dirty dishes to the girl who served him.

He lit a cigarette. The smell of grease now adhering to his clothes was far less attractive than before he ate. 'A tramp,' he thought. 'What possible motive was there? The same as in any murder,' he answered himself. He was convinced this was no random attack although he could not say why. Perhaps it was the unlikeliness of a stranger wandering in off the street. A psycho could have stabbed him, it was true, but surely he would not have returned and beaten him about the head with a brick. Peregrine Danvers, Harry Ford and John Cotton were adamant that blow came later. Even Ian, with his mediocre knowledge of such things, knew it to be so.

He was not given any longer to ponder the matter. Barry Swan came in just as he was stubbing out his cigarette and took the chair alongside the desk. He sat, arms draped over the back of it. At twenty-nine he was living proof that baldness was hereditary. His pale, blond hair was swept back over a domed crown, the scalp visible through the strands. To compensate he

24

wore the back longer, an inch or so over his collar. His lack of height was another hardship. In Ian's company he sat as often as he was able in order to hide the seven-inch discrepancy. To make up for what he considered to be handicaps he dressed with sartorial elegance, his clothes always the latest fashion. Ian and Moira had discussed it once. Moira believed his reputation for womanising was the result of his constant need for reassurance that he was attractive. He was still living this reputation down even though he had been seeing Lucy, and only Lucy, for many months.

'Made any sense of it?' Barry wanted to know.

'No. Do they ever make sense?'

'Sometimes. Heat of the moment. Drugs. Self-defence.'

'You know what I mean.'

'I'm not in for one of your philosophical discourses, am I?'

The Chief shook his head just as DC Campbell stuck his head round the door, rapping it with his knuckles at the same time.

'I've got the duty sergeant organised, sir. I ran a check on the whisky. No record of any Bell's being nicked. Want me for anything else?'

'No. When the statements start coming in, do your usual, will you?'

'Yes, sir.' DC Campbell's fascination with computers was well known. He was able to use them to their full advantage which meant everyone was happy, especially the Chief who disliked the idea of them but recognised their value.

'He must've bought the hooch yesterday. He'd hardly keep it for a special occasion, which means he probably only got the money yesterday. Any luck with the DSS?'

'They're doing their best.' Barry knew by the Chief's tone what that meant. But they could hardly be expected to come up with much without a name to work on.

'Was he blackmailing someone?'

'It crossed my mind. Good enough reason to get rid of him.'

'Oh, I forgot. Forensics have finished with him. Post-mortem's scheduled for tomorrow. The mortuary said they'll ring and let you know the time.'

'I'm sure they will.'

Barry grinned. Attending PMs was not the Chief's favourite occupation. 'Won't be another Barney Jones.'

The Chief smiled back, remembering a case several years ago where a man, similar to theirs, had been knocked down by a hit-and-run driver. Between the layers of clothes were discovered forty or fifty banknotes, almost unrecognisable they were so filthy. At one time he had been claiming benefits; he just didn't bother to spend them.

'We'll have to do the missing person bit – might as well get on to it now. You and Campbell. He's brilliant with the technology but he doesn't have your nose.' The Chief thought the task was pointless but no stone could be left unturned. It did not take an expert to tell the dead man was no recently missing person. It took years of living rough to look as he did. Fingerprints had been taken. It was only to be hoped that he had a record. At least the problem of his identity would be solved.

Meanwhile Barry was seated alongside DC Alan Campbell. He liked working with him, he was solid and reliable and not inclined to talk too much, but since the break-up with his wife he had become even more taciturn, occasionally morose.

Alan Campbell acknowledged Barry's presence with little more than a grunt. Barry, realising that no further conversation was to be forthcoming, lit a cigarette and picked up the first of the reports from a foot patrolman.

26

3

When Ian Roper pulled into Belmont Terrace most of the parking spaces had been taken. His three-bedroomed terraced house did not boast a garage but nevertheless had, since the day he and Moira moved into it, been home. Together, over the years, they had modernised and decorated it but it was Moira who saw to the garden. To Ian, gardens were somewhere to sit with a glass of wine at hand whilst he read the paper. He could just about recognise runner beans and roses; that was the extent of his horticultural interest.

He cruised to the far end of the street and parked on the corner, far enough away from the junction not to be a hazard. His journey home had been painless, the traffic light. It was the quiet time of evening, too late for most people to be returning from work, too early to be going out.

Darkness had fallen an hour or so ago and the street lights threw their sodium glow over the cars, making their colours seem other than what they were. Ian locked the car and automatically checked the handle before walking back towards number 14. Stars winked in a cloudless sky hinting at an early frost and the hum of traffic on the bypass carried faintly through the still air. The starlings were silent now.

There was a welcoming glow of light through the stained-glass fanlight window and from a chink in the living-room curtains. Moira was on the settee, feet beneath her, reading. A cup of coffee perched precariously on the arm. She saw by her husband's expression what kind of day he'd had.

'You're not as late as I expected,' she said, referring to the telephone call he'd made earlier. He always rang if he was going to be late. One of the reasons their marriage worked so well was because neither forgot the small courtesies that smoothed the way through difficult times.

Ian headed straight for the sideboard and poured a small measure of Scotch with the idea of unwinding. Seeing the bottle, although a different brand, brought back the trials of the day.

Moira, sensing his mood, picked up his car keys from where he'd dropped them on the chair, and placed them without comment on the hall table which was their agreed home. He was forever losing them but now was not the time to remind him of his forgetful habits. When she returned he was sitting in his armchair staring thoughtfully at the blank television screen.

'It just doesn't add up. What on earth would a vagrant do to make someone want to kill him?'

She did not ask if someone had; he would not be thinking aloud if it was not the case. 'Unintentionally maybe? A fight or something?'

'No. No sign of a struggle. Sorry, love, I didn't mean to bring it home with me.'

'You know I don't mind.' It was true. He used Moira as his sounding board and there had been times when she was able to see things from a different angle because she had none of the facts in front of her. 'Want anything to eat?'

'I had a meal earlier. I wouldn't mind something on toast though.'

'Poached eggs?'

'Fine.'

28

While the eggs were cooking and the bread was in the toaster, Moira stared at her own reflection in the blackness of the glass of the kitchen window. It was some time now since Ian had been on a murder inquiry. She knew what she was in for and hoped they would come through it unscathed. Her patience had been tried to the limit at times but she mostly bit her tongue, knowing that it wouldn't last, that Ian's job meant more to him than many people could imagine. He had admitted that his views were idealistic, possibly even old-fashioned, but he wanted to make the world a safer place.

She heard the toaster click off and buttered the toast, placing an egg on each of the slices. She carried the snack through to the living-room on a tray.

'Thanks,' he said, taking the tray from her. 'Two people.' He sighed, cut off a corner of the toast and dipped it in the egg. Moira waited for the explanation which would come, no doubt, when he'd finished eating.

'I enjoyed that . . . Two people tried to kill our man – we don't even know his name yet. First he was stabbed, then after he was dead, someone fractured his skull for him.'

'And you don't think it's the same person?'

'No. Too much of a time gap, and different methods. There's no sign of the knife but the brick was still there.'

'I . . . Oh, really. How many times have I told him to do things quietly?' Moira said as the front door crashed shut, causing the living-room door to vibrate.

'Hi, aged parents. No telly?'

'Dad's only just got in.' She gave him a warning glance. Mark knew from experience what that meant. He suffered as much as his mother at certain times.

'I think I'll go to my room.'

Ian, the better for the whisky and some food inside him, said, 'No need. Put it on if you want.'

'The solution might be to buy me one of my own.'

'We'll see. Maybe for Christmas,' Moira interjected before this particular argument could gain ground. They had given in and got him a computer last year and felt that he spent far too much time with it. There was a time when Mark had been sullen and uncooperative, when, much as she loved him, she was glad of his absence. Now, at seventeen and with successful GCSE results behind him, he was again the cheerful, outgoing boy he used to be.

They compromised on a film which had started ten minutes before: Ian flatly refused to watch a popular detective series and he could hardly inflict football on them after saying that. His mind was working overtime but, despite his natural inclination to go over the day's events, he found himself concentrating on the film.

'They didn't say much on the local news, did they?' Moira said as she brushed her fair, shoulder-length hair before getting into bed.

'There's not a lot they can say. Just the usual press release. We weren't even being cagey, they know as much as we do.'

DC Alan Campbell refused Barry's offer of a quick drink after work. He was aware that he was in danger of becoming a recluse since his wife had left but he still wasn't up to socialising. It had hit him hard but he did not let it affect his work. His father's influence had left its mark. Brought up by strict, puritanical Scottish parents, he had not been allowed to indulge in self-pity. He had inherited their attitudes and their looks. Alan's sandy hair, blue eyes and almost white complexion left no one in doubt of his origins even before he spoke. He had grown a moustache to try to disguise the thinness of his face but he still looked as if he was in need of a decent meal. It was only a few months before Helen left

30

him that he had been moved to CID from the uniform branch. His pride in this achievement kept him going. That and the pleasure he got from computers. He said good-night to Barry. 'Another time,' he added, knowing he must soon make the effort, then he returned to the two-bedroomed house he and Helen once shared. There was nothing of her left in it now. Surfaces where ornaments had stood were bare, the bathroom cabinet and wardrobe half empty. It was better that way. The austerity suited him.

Barry Swan sighed. They had all failed to get Alan back in circulation. He returned to his own bachelor flat but it was quite a different place. Many women had spent time there. Until the advent of Lucy. He grinned as he parked the car. He had been glad when some of his one-night stands had gone home; the morning after could leave a bad taste. With Lucy he wanted her there all the time. It was she who refused.

He climbed the stairs to his first-floor accommodation, seeing no one, hearing nothing. It was that kind of genteel property. Even now, after five years, he was grateful to his grandmother each time he returned to it. On his salary it would have taken years to afford such a place. In a typically eccentric letter left with her solicitors pending the time of her death, she explained that as she did not get on with her own children and, likewise, they had little time for her, she saw no reason why they should benefit from her death. She left the flat and a few thousand pounds she had saved to her grandson.

Barry hung his olive green trenchcoat on a hanger, straightening the collar as he did so, then, feeling lazy, put a ready-made beef dinner in the microwave. He poured a can of lager to go with it.

'PC Walters needs his arse kicked,' he thought, waiting for the foam to subside in his glass. 'He had enough sense to realise our man had been murdered, but not enough to detain the man who found him.' Barry had a good idea of how Walters' sergeant would handle the matter. It was likely he would come down harder on him than was necessary due to his own shortcomings, for not spotting that one of his men was an idle bugger.

He chewed his food without really tasting it. Like his boss, he took a while to switch off from the job. Markham had discovered that the bottle of Bell's was purchased in the off-licence in Bradley Rise, a road midway between the High Street and where the tramp slept. The counter staff knew him by sight because he bought the occasional bottle of cider. They called him Charlie but could not say whether or not this was his real name. The woman Markham interviewed had said he was never any trouble, just a bit on the smelly side. Barry smiled. She was not given to hyperbole.

It was also unlikely that the post-mortem would pick up anything they had missed. Harry Ford from the Home Office suggested the spleen was ruptured. The cause of death must be the stab wounds. It was the head injury which was baffling. What purpose did it serve?

Barry, as tidy in his home as he was in his appearance, threw the food container into the pedal bin and washed his few dishes before looking at the paper to see if there was anything worth watching on the television. He couldn't stand football, the film was a repeat and he was definitely not in the mood for a smartass crime-solving detective. He flicked through his large collection of CDs but decided to go out instead. He checked his pockets for wallet and keys and went out into the darkness wishing that Lucy was with him.

'Nothing else then?' Detective Chief Inspector Roper rubbed his temples with thumb and forefinger. He had not slept well. Nothing to do with the case this time;

Moira was developing a cold and kept switching on the bedside lamp in search of tissues or a sip of water. His glance at the incident book had been cursory.

'Just this, sir,' the desk sergeant said. 'Another heroin addict.' It was the fourth time in several weeks that that drug had come up.

'It had to happen sooner or later, I suppose.' The Chief sighed. Situated where it was, Rickenham Green did not have the drug epidemics rife in the cities. Everything caught up eventually but for once he was thankful to be behind the times. 'Has someone been sent to the hospital?'

'The ward sister said there was no point until later. The girl's too far gone to be questioned. She's not a registered addict though. She got herself to casualty last night, climbing the walls apparently, and demanding police protection.'

'Get someone to follow it up, will you?'

In his office the Chief prepared the morning's briefing and read through his own handwritten notes.

A few more pieces of information had been placed on his desk sometime since his departure the previous evening. It was confirmed that the tramp had been killed in the spot where he was found and it could be presumed he toppled over when the head wound was inflicted. Forensics were working on samples of clothing etc., but there was still no clue to the man's identity. True, every killer leaves a little of himself behind but, without anything with which to match it, the information was useless.

The interviewing of the homeless of Rickenham continued and the media appeals for information were in motion. The *Rickenham Herald* was not due out for another two days but Martyn Bright, the editor, was coming over later for the details.

The case, although only a day old, had brought its

rewards. In the search of derelict buildings for possible witnesses, two fifteen-year-old schoolboys who were playing truant were found glue-sniffing. They were returned to their shocked and angry parents who, hopefully, now they were aware of the circumstances, would not allow them to be repeated. In the long grass behind the flats a carrier bag containing three blouses nicked from Dorothy Perkins at the weekend was found. The bag was not particularly hidden; the culprit must have panicked and dumped it.

Some of the vagrants were incoherent, others were garrulous, none was able to be of assistance. Most of them were approached in the streets; one or two, who initially seemed to know something, were brought in for questioning. The interview rooms stank of air freshener.

As the Chief crossed the main foyer to check a few facts regarding another case, DS Markham came through the swing doors almost pushing the man ahead of him. He could have been the dead man's double, except he was a little younger. Markham's expression spoke volumes and his eyes glittered. The Chief suspected he had been made a fool of.

'I'm not under arrest, am I?' the man asked.

'You might be, if you're not a bit more co-operative,' Markham replied.

'I'll take over,' the Chief interrupted, frowning coldly. He would speak to Markham later. He might be the exception which proved the rule as far as policemen went, but there was no need for rough handling in this instance.

The Chief led the man along the corridor to a vacant interview room. 'Please sit down. I hope you haven't been inconvenienced, but we are investigating a murder.'

'I'm fully aware of that?' His head was on one side, posing a question.

'Chief Inspector Roper. May I know your name and, er, details?' Address was hardly the appropriate description.

'Naturally. How refreshing to find a police officer with manners.'

The Chief shuddered. So much for public image. The man's tone was almost derisive as he said, 'My name is William Golding.' The Chief sighed and began to sympathise with Markham. Was this one of the local nutters? On second thoughts, the name Golding would possibly mean nothing to Markham, who did not come across as a reader of literature. Golding studied the man opposite him and correctly guessed his thoughts.

'Coincidence,' he said. 'I do not claim to be, nor to have any relationship to, that author. If I had been born with that talent and used a pen to earn my living I might not be in the predicament I am now. And I am in a predicament, aren't I, Chief Inspector?' His smile was wry.

In turn the Chief studied Golding, but did not reply immediately.

'It's all right, I'm not insane, merely impecunious.'

The Chief believed him and wished, not for the first time, that there were enough hours in the day to be able to talk to people from different walks of life. Not question or interrogate, but really talk, to find out what made them tick. 'Did you know the deceased?'

'Yes. And it was I who reported finding him.' The Chief's interest was doubled. 'Once I was sure Charlie was dead I set off to find a constable. There's usually one around at that time of day, head in the clouds if you ask me, but that's your affair. He didn't seem particularly interested. I won't repeat his actual words, but he took some convincing that he ought to have a look.'

'But . . .'

William Golding held up an apologetic hand.

'I know what you're going to ask. I'm sorry, but I must admit that once I'd told him I made myself scarce. I discovered I had the British trait of not wanting to get involved. I also thought he might suspect me. However, after sleeping on it I decided to come here. I was actually on my way when your sergeant found me and hastened my arrival.'

'Was Charlie his real name?'

'That I couldn't tell you. We never really discussed our backgrounds, not in any depth. Some things are better left unknown. However, we knew each other as well as any two people can who share the same sleeping arrangements and the same problem, but I don't know any reason why anyone would want him dead.'

'The same problem? What might that be, Mr Golding?'

'Ah, too great an enjoyment of things better taken in moderation. Namely, alcohol.'

'Charlie was alcoholic?'

Golding laughed. 'No. None of us is that, we can't afford to be.'

'I see. And the others who share your sleeping arrangements, were you all together on Monday night?' The Chief was unconsciously parodying Golding's manner of speech. It was a long time since he had interviewed someone who spoke in sentences.

'We were all there, except Charlie. At the time no one took any notice. Charlie was a greedy man. If he had a good day he might purchase a drink but he would not share it. If it was anyone else he expected them to do so.'

'And did they share it?'

'Yes, mostly.'

'And if not, did Charlie lose his temper?'

Golding shook his head. 'Not that I ever saw. I don't understand it. If Charlie had any problems I'm sure he would have told me.'

'What was his surname, Mr Golding?'

Golding looked surprised. 'I have no idea.'

'Didn't you ask?'

'No. When you live as we do these things lose their importance.'

'When did you last see him alive?'

'Early on Monday afternoon. He said he was going to St Hilda's Walk. The Town Hall's his usual spot. We each keep to our own places, it saves any squabbling. Besides, if people see you in pairs they become intimidated. Yes, that was the last time I saw him. Until Tuesday morning, of course.' Golding's mouth tightened as if he was trying to suppress the memory.

It seemed as if their theory was correct. They knew Charlie had returned to the waste ground sometime during Monday evening but he had not been visible to his companions.

'I have to ask you, Mr Golding, did you kill Charlie?'

Golding laughed out loud. It was a deep, pleasant sound, but he seemed surprised, as if he was not used to hearing it. 'Me? Kill anyone? Do I strike you as that type of man?'

The Chief did not reply. Any type of man could kill with enough provocation.

'Thank you for your help. Do you wish to make a complaint against Detective Sergeant Markham?'

There was fresh laughter in Golding's eyes. 'Do you really think that would be a wise move?'

There was no answer to that. 'Actually, I think your man's main objection was to having me in his car. I mean,' he indicated his greasy coat, 'it can't have been pleasant.'

'Perhaps not,' the Chief said, smiling back. He had left the interview room door ajar for that very reason. He rose and showed Golding out, accompanying him back along the corridor.

'Mr Golding, I was wondering . . .'

'You were wondering how I got myself into this situation.'

'Yes. Excuse my curiosity.'

'It was the usual story. I was born with intelligence and given a good education. I wasted both. I trained as a medical student but unfortunately I have what is known in the trade as an addictive personality. I drank to get a good night's sleep, then I drank because I needed to. One thing led to another. Drugs were relatively easy to come by. I took them. Eventually I was struck off. I can't blame the authorities. I went downhill fast from there, I lost everything. At least I can't afford drugs now, even if I knew where to obtain them. Most of the time I don't have the funds for a drink.'

They were at the revolving doors in the main entrance through which Golding had made his undignified appearance. 'Don't feel sorry for me, Chief Inspector,' he said. 'That's the last thing you should do. It's all of my own making.' And with that he was gone. Fresh, cool air wafted in as the doors revolved silently.

'So that's the Sir William character,' Ian said, as he related the events to Barry.

'Classic case by the sound of it. Drink and drugs and rock and roll.'

'Mm. At least we know Charlie's movements up to the early part of the evening. It checks out with what the woman in the off-licence said. He must have gone straight there after leaving St Hilda's Walk. Golding said he was a greedy man. How greedy, I wonder? It might be an idea to question some of those office workers, could be something there. Have a couple of people there as they're leaving work.'

Barry went to organise this and left the Chief making a few notes of his own. When Ian returned to his own office he found Doc Harris waiting.

'Missed out on a stiff, did I?'

Ian raised his eyebrows. 'News travels fast.'

'I'm just passing through. Had to hand in a report. I wondered if you and Moira fancied coming over for a drink and some supper tonight. Shirley said to ask. She'd never forgive me if I forgot.'

'It's not on, I'm afraid. There's no telling what time I'll finish.'

'Oh, well, another time. Better get back to the surgery.'

Ian grinned as he watched him leave. Round-shouldered, seedy, his fingers nicotine-stained – it did not matter. His sense of humour and his sense of the order of things remained intact. Ian thought he was one of the nicest people he had the pleasure to know.

The smile did not last. Reading a note on his desk from DC Campbell, he learned that Charlie's fingerprints were not on record. There was, however, a sheet containing his dental record. Surprisingly, only three teeth were missing.

'Here,' he said, shoving both pieces of paper across the desk at Barry when he returned bearing two mugs of coffee.

Barry was equally pessimistic. 'I don't suppose he's seen a dentist in years. But you never know.'

Ian thought he did know. He thought a lot of time and energy would be wasted circulating copies to all the local dentists who would then waste their time going through their records. However, if it meant a minimal chance of proving his identity it had to be done.

'Get it copied, Barry. And tell Markham I want a word, would you?'

'What's he been up to now? Doing his prima donna act again?'

Ian did not respond. He refused to discuss his men's shortcomings with anyone but the person concerned. Praise, however, he was quick to pass on.

'Sir?'

'Come in, Markham.' He did not invite him to sit down. 'Mr Golding. You're lucky he's not going to make a complaint.'

'Yes, sir.'

'Is that all you have to say? Yes, sir? Are you aware of my opinion of that sort of behaviour? And not only my opinion, that of Superintendent Thorne and any other officer who treats their work the way it should be treated.'

'I'm sorry, sir. It won't happen again.'

'Make sure it doesn't. You can go now.'

Markham did so. He was not in the least upset; he knew it was coming to him. He was not a man to make excuses. Only he would ever know that Golding had laid into him verbally, using his superior education to make him feel small, stating his opinion of the police, especially men like Markham, in no uncertain terms. He should not have reacted. He knew his intellectual limits and they were greater than most people believed. By the time he was downstairs the incident was out of his mind.

Just as Markham's mood was brightening, Barry's was doing the reverse. He had telephoned Lucy and was annoyed to learn she had not been available last night because she preferred to go to the cinema with her flatmates. She accused him of possessiveness and told him that her life did not, nor ever would, revolve around one man. The problem was, she explained it so reasonably. He was the one behaving unreasonably and he knew it, which did not improve his temper. For the first time in his life the good-looking, womanising Barry Swan found the boot to be firmly on the other foot.

'Don't sulk,' Lucy said just before she put the phone down. 'Ring me later.'

Ian found himself thinking about William Golding and how it must feel for someone highly trained to sink to such depths. Drugs. He hated the very word. It was a constant worry that Mark might get into the wrong company. So far they had been lucky. He didn't even like Ian smoking, a habit which was taken up and given up with monotonous regularity.

He doodled on a piece of paper as he decided what to do next. The search of the waste ground for the murder weapon was at an end and house-to-house inquiries in that part of town were next to useless. But they had to be seen to be doing something.

The homeless had been rounded up – there were more than Ian thought possible. He allowed himself a smirk as he read the report handed in by the young PC who had had the misfortune to come across Mad Dora. She was going through the contents of a litter bin at the time. She talked incessantly and what she had to say bore no relation to reality or to the questions being asked her. Her main concern was to get her interviewer to eat the offerings she produced from a tattered shopping bag. 'Dora wants you to have this,' was the most sensible thing she said.

Ian decided it was time to get something to eat himself.

The office workers, hurrying towards the car-park or buses, were not thrilled to have to stop and answer questions. Many remembered the tramp but few were certain when they last saw him. The general reaction was that it was probably Monday. They were used to his presence, but the questions were asked not so much to

41

ascertain when he was last seen, that much was already known, but whether anything unusual had occurred. It seemed it had not.

'All we have to do, then,' Barry said, still stinging from his telephone conversation with Lucy, 'is to find out what he was up to during the next four hours.'

'No need for sarcasm. We'll get there in the end.' But this was not certain. Most people, whatever their position in life, followed some sort of routine. Even a man or woman in a lonely bedsit might have a neighbour who could add to the general picture. For want of inspiration they were calling the investigation 'Operation Charlie'. 'Which is what we're all going to look like if we don't come up with something soon,' Ian said, beginning to be affected by Barry's grouchiness.

He looked at the clock on the wall. It was after seven. Norwich City would be out on the pitch warming up. Typical of his luck. After years of following them, getting to every conceivable match, now they had started to do so well he wasn't getting a chance to watch them. Except that one blissful occasion when he had a ticket to see them play Bayern Munich. He was there. He would never forget the feeling when Valencia scored for Bayern in the fourth minute. But he was also there to rise with the rest of the Carrow Road crowd when Goss scored in the fifty-first minute. Norwich had won 3-2 on aggregate. It was a moment he would remember for the rest of his life. He could not recall a time when he had not supported them, even though he was Suffolk born and bred and it would have been more logical to support Ipswich, whose ground was nearer, and more loyal to his county. However, work dictated that he could not always attend. Tonight Norwich would have to cope as best they could without him.

WPC Judy Robbins was chatting to the desk sergeant when he decided to call it a day. For reasons which were not clear to either of them, theirs was an easy, comfortable relationship considering the distance between their ranks. Judy was on the plump side and could not really be called attractive. But she had an open, honest face, clear skin and very thick, dark hair which Ian thought it was a pity she kept so short. There was no sexual attraction but a companionship which developed because they both wanted the same things out of the job and out of life. Judy's mother had died when she was a child. A few years ago she had moved to her own place, fearing she might never leave home otherwise, because her father, now retired, made life too cosy. Used to fending for himself, he cooked and cleaned. She still saw a lot of him but knew she had made a wise decision.

'I was going to ring you, sir. I've just got back from Rickenham General. The girl's gone. The junkie.'

'Discharged?'

'No, disappeared. The ward sister said we could speak to her. When I arrived she was nowhere to be found. Seems odd when it was her who wanted protection from us. I mean, she can't have been abducted from a hospital bed.'

'Damn. Presumably they've got her details. I want her found.'

'I've got the name and address. I was just about to check it out.'

'Good. No need to ring tonight. Tomorrow morning'll be soon enough.'

He said good-night and headed for his car. In the car-park Doc Harris was bending over the wing of his Jaguar examining the paintwork. It was by no means a new car but it was a cherished possession. Chrome and paintwork gleamed and the leather seats were soft from years of wear. 'What brings you back again?'

'Had to come in for a blood sample. Drink/driving. Too darn dark to tell. What do you think?' Momentarily

43

he removed a cigarette from between his lips. He was never observed lighting up yet always managed to have a half-smoked stub in his mouth.

Ian looked at the off-side wing. 'Can't see anything myself. I'm assuming you're looking for some minute scratch.' Ian left him gazing sadly at the car and went home.

4

The man in the suit watched and waited. At first it was a relief. There was no sign of the tramp on Tuesday or Wednesday. Then reality struck home. The tramp was dead and he had killed him. He did not, could not, allow himself to think of that possibility until then. What he had done was for a good reason, everything he'd done recently was for the same reason, for the one person he loved. He had made a mistake, a very foolish one which he could not justify, even to himself. What it had led to was far worse, dragging him down to the depths until he had no control whatsoever. He no longer felt like a man.

By Wednesday he was surprised no one had commented on his appearance. Surely the anxiety was etched in his face. Maybe not. The tension had been there for many months now. Probably it no longer showed.

One consoling thought kept him going. The wounds he had inflicted on the tramp might only have injured him and served as a warning, which was what he had intended. He must continue to wait, but for how long? He knew he was near breaking point.

Markham, with an untidy flat to go home to, remained at the station. Eventually he would have a good clean-up but as he was hardly ever there and never took visitors back, it did not seem to matter.

He had been, and as no one had told him otherwise, presumably still was, the officer in charge of a warehouse robbery. It had taken place almost a month ago. Many hours of interviewing and slogging footwork had served no purpose. The case remained unsolved. As it had to be an inside job it was doubly frustrating. Yet every member of staff had an unbreakable alibi or was squeaky clean or did not have access to the information needed to complete the job so successfully. Of course, someone, somewhere had to be lying; the problem was finding out who. More annoying, especially to Markham, was that the goods must be long gone. Not one of his informers came up with anything. There were no illicit video recorders or camcorders on the streets of Rickenham Green. Having the distraction of Operation Charlie he might now, at a distance, be able to see something he missed.

He accessed the information from the computer and studied the screen and it was then the idea struck him. The warehouse was only a matter of yards from the spot where Charlie's body was found. Was it possible he had seen something and for that reason been silenced? Charlie was no longer able to say, but if this was the case then solving one crime would also solve the other.

With his usual grim determination he reread every statement taken at the time.

As Markham read, a block of flats behind the Station Arms was being burgled. It was not an uncommon event. Two uniformed PCs left the comfortable warmth of their car in response and went to investigate. PCs Jackson and Stone, long partnered but with an age gap large enough for them to have been father and son,

46

sighed when they heard their destination. 'Why do they bother?' Jackson asked rhetorically as he parked the car in a place where he hoped it would be safe. 'There can't be anything left worth taking.'

They walked towards the building. It would be a waste of time. It always was. Security here was particularly poor and the inhabitants frequently careless. The building, when new, was the tallest in the town. Seven storeys high. It was erected in the early sixties by the council, at a time when its members were not unknown to take holidays abroad at the expense of the developers whose tender they accepted. It was shoddily built and its condition deteriorated rapidly. Because it was such a soulless, depressing place to live in, it was not surprising that the residents took little pride in their surroundings.

From the police point of view there was too much coming and going, too much indifference; and with forty families, most with children or teenagers, it was impossible for a resident to monitor the movements of someone who had no business there.

An opportunist only had to watch for someone to go out then force the inadequate lock. Neighbours here minded their own business.

The walls of the entrance hall were covered with graffiti, some of it quite imaginative, if misspelled. The predominant aroma was urine. Three youths lounged against the wall, bored and listless. They tried to exude menace but it was lost on Jackson and Stone.

'Filth,' one of them said, spitting on the floor, not brave enough to sully a uniform.

'Filth is right,' PC Stone commented. 'And if I didn't have better things to do I'd make you clean up that mess.'

'Pigs,' another youth muttered as the lift doors opened.

47

'Past your bedtime, isn't it, lads?' Jackson parried just as the doors closed.

'Thank God my lot are grown up,' Frank Stone said. 'I just hope the grandchildren don't turn out like that.'

The first flat broken into was on the third floor and belonged to a woman in her early sixties. 'I'd been to the bingo,' she told them. 'I got home a bit before my usual time because I got a line up and treated myself to a taxi. It's daft, you know – they build a place like this for all us people and there's no bus stop handy. Still, I'm glad the little beggars didn't wait until tomorrow.' They knew better than to ask why. Mrs Bennet, the lady in question, was of the school that believed it was foolish to trust your money to banks or building societies. Hard cash in her handbag was what she liked, or maybe some notes hidden in a biscuit tin.

'I got back about half an hour ago. You've been quick, haven't you?'

'We were in the area, madam.'

'Oh. Well, I saw the door was open a bit and realised what had happened. I didn't come in, in case they were still here, like, so I got Mr Singh from across the passage to come with me. He's a good neighbour, despite what some people might think, quiet like, except I don't know how he can wear that turban thing all the time, must make his head itch something awful. Anyway, no one was here so he let me use his telephone. Look at it.' She swept her arm in an arc indicating the mess. On the floor were the contents of drawers and cupboards. Patiently they waited whilst she made a list of missing items.

'Are you insured?' PC Jackson inquired.

'What on earth for? The payments'd cost more than all my bits and pieces put together.'

There were tears in her eyes when she discovered a ring her husband had given her was missing. 'It was all I'd got to remember him by.'

48

They did not like to leave her alone but she insisted she was quite all right. 'They'll not be back again, they've seen it's not worth their while. And Mr Singh's going to fix up the door for me, he said he'd wait until you'd gone. Oh, take no notice of that,' Mrs Bennet continued as muffled thuds were heard through the thin walls. 'Those two are always at it hammer and tongs, and if you ask me, it's him what usually comes off worse.' There was the sound of crockery breaking, which prompted her to ask if they wanted a cup of tea. They refused politely and walked up one flight of stairs to the fourth floor.

An enlarged eye peered out through a spyhole before the door opened. This sop to security had not prevented the grubby man who stood before them from being robbed. He was the same age as Mrs Bennet but looked ten years her senior. The room was overheated and smelled of sweat and stale tobacco. The sound of a wailing child echoed down the corridor. PC Stone supposed the residents must become used to the noise.

'Come in, then,' the man said. 'I got back from the pub and found this lot. I've mended the door. Didn't think you'd bother taking fingerprints, you don't usually round here.'

Drawers and cupboards hung open, their contents scattered around in much the same way as in the flat below, except here it was obvious that the thieves were not responsible for all the mess. George Miller was by no means the cleanest of men. It did not take much detection to conclude the robberies were the work of the same person or persons.

Miller's story was identical. He returned home to find the door open.

'Do you know what's missing?' PC Stone asked.

'Not a great deal, I shouldn't think.' He fingered the tide-marked collar of his shirt. The skin around his throat

49

was grey and stringy and his Adam's apple bobbed up and down nervously as he spoke. Despite his blasé attitude he was probably upset; it was not a pleasant thing to happen. George Miller lit a cigarette and coughed long and wetly, not bothering to cover his mouth. When the spasm was over he said, 'Digital alarm clock's gone, wasn't worth much. Can't've been. It was a present from my boy and he's skint.'

'If you wouldn't mind having a quick look around, sir, see if anything else is missing. Maybe later, when you've tidied up a bit, you can contact us if you discover other items gone.'

Miller cast his eyes around the room. 'There was a couple of quid in loose change in this bowl – no more'n three pounds, I shouldn't think. For the electric. Oh, my radio.' This loss obviously hurt. 'I only got it in Curry's sale a few weeks ago. It's one of those modern things, what d'you call them? Ghetto blasters, is it? You can't get a good old-fashioned radio nowadays. I always listen to the sport on it, beats the telly every time.' He turned to rummage in a drawer. 'Here . . .' He thrust some crumpled paper towards them. 'Receipt and my part of the guarantee.'

Jackson made a note of the details. The guarantee was a blanket one to cover all the goods manufactured by the electrical company. Miller had had the good sense to jot down the serial number. 'We don't need these but the insurance people might. Anything more?'

Miller hesitated for a fraction of a second. 'No,' he said, 'nothing more.'

'We'll be in touch if we hear anything. Will you be okay?'

'Course I will.'

'Good-night then, sir.'

They knocked on neighbouring doors on both the fourth and third floors. Those that were in had not heard or seen anything. 'Hardly surprising with all that bloody row going on,' PC Stone commented as they returned to the car. 'TVs blaring, kids screeching. Jesus, it would drive a man to drink.'

'Something bothering you back there, Frank?' PC Jackson asked.

'Maybe, maybe not. Miller seemed nervous. Understandable in the circumstances, but he had a couple of video cassettes stuffed down the side of the settee. It's a wonder they weren't taken. But there was no recorder. And the shelf under the TV. Empty, not even a newspaper, but every other surface was a mess. Odd, that's all, there being an empty space when the rest of the place was a tip.'

'Perhaps he flogged it, or didn't like it and took it back to the rental people. Could be that's how he could afford the radio.'

'Hm,' Frank Stone muttered as he got into the passenger seat.

Their report would indicate that the stolen items were small enough to be have been taken out of the building without arousing suspicion. It was unlikely they would ever be recovered.

Their shift was almost over. They were conscientious men, alert to the end of it. They might even come across the youngsters responsible, for the job had the trademark of youngsters.

On Wednesday nights there was free admission to the Nite Spot for accompanied females if they took the trouble to cut out a coupon from the previous week's *Rickenham Herald*. It was an establishment where loud music and flashing lights predominated and whose exorbitant price for a pint of lager made the older, beer-drinking contingency of the town laugh at the gullibility of youth. There would be trouble later. There always was. Too much alcohol, someone dancing with someone

51

else's girlfriend, these things were enough to instigate a fight.

'Remember that last one?' Jackson reminisced as they watched the crocodile of scruffily dressed teenagers queuing to get in. 'The one who wouldn't take no for an answer?'

'I do indeed.' PC Stone laughed. 'So bloody determined to get into that hell-hole he took a flying leap at the doors. Plate glass, the idiot. Wouldn't take no from the bouncers. Can't understand it myself. You'd have to pay *me* to go into a place like that. Now, when I was a youngster . . .'

'Not now, Frank, if you don't mind. I think I've got one of my headaches coming on.'

PC Stone glanced at his companion's profile but could not decide if he was serious.

DS Markham had given up. It seemed he had not overlooked anything. He was sitting in the canteen, brooding, a mug of black coffee in front of him, when WPC Judy Robbins joined him, uninvited. As far as he liked anyone, he liked Judy. They were two of a kind in a way. Solitary figures who enjoyed their own company and their work. Judy was honest and assertive. Many of her male colleagues mistook these qualities for aggression. Markham took them at their face value. He had no hang-ups about equality, it was a concept which did not concern him. He either liked someone or he didn't. Mostly he didn't. He did not fancy Judy, she was too tall and too plump for his taste, but her company was welcome.

'What's up, Markham?' Judy plonked herself inelegantly into the chair opposite, spilling coffee as she did so.

'Nothing really.'

She pushed a thick lock of hair back from her forehead and undid the top button of her blouse. Another day was almost over.

'Nothing really? What does that mean? Someone breathing down your neck?'

'No. The Chief had a few words to say.'

'The Chief?' she was surprised. He was a fair man who treated his staff well and didn't bollock them unless it was absolutely necessary. He was one of her favourite people but she suspected it was because he reminded her of her father. Ian would not have liked to know that.

'I deserved it. After twenty-four hours of disgustingly filthy old men I overstepped the mark.' Even to Judy he made no excuses.

'Ah, Operation Charlie.'

'Yes. No progress. I stayed on to go over the JC Warehousing files. Nothing there either. Bit of a dead loss all round. Want another coffee?'

'No thanks. Got to go. I'm having the last hour down the pub with Dad. It's his darts night.'

'See you.'

Markham finished his own coffee and decided to find his snout. He, too, would have a few drinks. He was officially off duty. He often frequented the haunts of known villains, and although his *modus operandi* was frowned upon it was ignored because of the results he got. It was no longer policy for CID to direct their inquiries in public houses. He walked briskly towards the Prince William, unable to take things slowly at any time. It was a shabby, back-street pub, renamed after the birth of a royal baby. Here, if you knew the right people, you could purchase almost anything from a fake Cartier watch to a lorry-load of frozen fish fingers. By quarter to ten his snout hadn't showed. He decided to call it a day.

Needing to empty his bladder he pushed open the door of the gents. It was evil at the best of times but tonight one of the more enthusiastic customers, unable to make it to the cubicle, was vomiting on the tiled floor. Markham decided he could wait.

By the time he reached the High Street he knew he couldn't. The cold wind was making matters worse. With a quick glance in both directions, he dived into the alley between Boots and Marks and Spencer where he unzipped his jeans and, with a sigh of relief, urinated against the wall.

PCs Jackson and Stone, on their way back to clock off, were still alert. Frank Stone spotted the figure diving into the alley. They stopped the car and approached cautiously, then realised the true situation.

A man dressed in jeans and leather jacket stood with his back to them. He was on the tall side, wide-shouldered, and he held himself well.

'Good evening, sir,' Jackson began. 'Are you aware that it's an offence . . .'

'Of course I am. I was taken short.'

'I see. And would you mind telling us where you've just come from?'

'Yes, I bloody well would.'

'Okay, we can do it the hard way, or we can do it the easy way. Your name?'

'Markham.'

Alarm bells sounded in their heads. It was too late now to back down.

'And your first names, sir?'

'Detective Sergeant.'

They should have recognised him, they knew him by sight, but the alley was very dark and they were chasing villains, not on the look-out for superior officers.

'In that case, we'll leave it at that. However, if you don't mind me saying, it's not very good for our image for the CID to be seen urinating in the streets. And it is still a criminal offence.'

'I'm suitably chastened,' Markham replied, secretly enjoying himself, 'but,' he added as he stepped back into the High Street, 'I feel a hundred per cent better for a piss.'

'Cocky bugger,' PC Stone muttered, unimpressed. 'You should've booked him anyway.'

'Maybe. But whatever else they say about him, he's no different from the rest of us biologically.' And with that profound thought they continued on their way to the station.

5

DCI Roper was more than surprised to find William Golding waiting in the reception area when he arrived early at work on Thursday morning. He raised a hand in greeting and continued to the desk.

'What's he doing here?' he asked, quietly enough to ensure that Golding would not hear.

'Waiting for you, sir. Refused to see anyone else. He's been there about twenty minutes.'

'Okay. I'll just get some tea. I'll buzz down when I'm ready. On second thoughts, I'll see him in an interview room.'

The desk sergeant smiled, guessing his reasons. Even from where he stood he could smell the man.

'Mr Golding, would you like to come through here?'

Golding followed him, no shuffling gait but a firm steady tread.

'I'm sorry to take up your time, Chief Inspector, but something came to mind which might be relevant.'

'Yes?' He mentally crossed his fingers, praying for a breakthrough.

'It may be nothing, but it was on Monday, the night before he died, that Charlie bought a bottle of whisky. I'm assuming he bought it. There was one near him.' He waited for Ian's nod then continued. 'The previous Monday he had a bottle too.'

'And?'

'Well, that's it, I'm afraid. Two Mondays in a row he was able to purchase whisky. Charlie was an observant man, he didn't miss much.'

'What are you suggesting, Mr Golding?' He knew but he wanted the man to say it.

'Not suggesting, merely opining. Blackmail, perhaps. However, anything else I say will only be speculation. I just felt you ought to know.'

'Thank you once again for coming. It may be useful information – time will tell.'

It had hardly been worth taking him into the interview room. He asked a passing PC to show Golding out and went up to his own office, unsure what to make of it.

'Sir?'

'Come in, Judy.'

The Chief watched her from under his brows. WPC Judy Robbins was biting her lower lip which meant she had her teeth into something, figuratively as well as physically.

'That girl, the one at the hospital, she gave a false name and address. We've been through the Register of Electors, amongst other things. There're four Debbie Wilkeses listed for Rickenham Green and the surrounding area. They all check out. I saw two last night, mother and daughter, the daughter's about the right age but definitely not our girl. The other two I saw this morning. A Mrs Wilkes in Bradley Court, in her mid-thirties with two young kiddies. The other happens to be a sister at Rickenham General. It could be the girl saw her name badge and said the first thing that came into her head when she was asked.'

'Could be,' the Chief said, tapping his desk with a pen, 'unless she knew the Debbie Wilkes you saw. If they are the same age they might've gone to school together. It's not unknown for girls to use each others' names.'

It was Judy's turn to smile. 'No. This one lives in Chestnut Avenue and attended Priory Towers. Pity the nurses couldn't remember what sort of accent our girl had. All they can say is that it certainly wasn't posh.'

'Hm. Priory Towers. That must have sent pater back a bob or two.' At one time he and Moira had toyed with the idea of sending Mark to a fee-paying school. Now they were glad they hadn't.

'Judging by the house, they can afford it. Anyway, I checked again with the hospital in case she returned. One of the student nurses told me that Debbie, or whatever her name is, saw a man in the ward entrance and looked terrified. He didn't enter the ward so the nurse didn't challenge him. She was in the middle of a nasogastric feed at the time and intended asking Debbie who he was. She said her back was turned for only a few minutes and that's when Debbie disappeared.'

'This man. How old?'

'She said about mid-twenties. Not much of a description either. Usual dress, you know, jeans, bomber jacket, baseball cap.'

'Oh, very useful. That covers eighty per cent of the young males in Rickenham.'

'Boyfriend, do you think? Or supplier?' Judy thought aloud.

'Could be either, or both. I want her found. I want this trash stamped out. How old did you say she is?'

'She gave her age as nineteen. The nursing staff said it was probably correct.'

'Can I leave it with you?'

'I can but try. Bit of a sod, sir, isn't it, neither of us having identification to go on.'

'Please. Don't remind me. Keep me informed, Judy.'

There were some crimes Ian could understand, one or two criminals he had a peculiar sort of respect for, but to him, drug dealers were the lowest form of life. If there was one in Rickenham he would have him. It was an instance where he was sorry he was not responsible for sentencing as well.

As there were enough people employed on Operation Charlie, Markham requested to be allowed to continue with the break-in at the warehouse. Permission was granted provided he was prepared to be pulled off if things hotted up. He tapped his code into the computer terminal and extracted the information he required: a list of crimes, no matter how minor, carried out in the area around the railway station. He was already aware of the burglaries at the flats the previous evening. Those flats had had many similar incidents in the past few weeks. The files were still open. He guessed they would remain that way. There were also two 'domestics' and one case of solvent abuse. These last did not seem serious enough to be connected with what he was after.

Nothing jumped out at him. For the second time in two days he reread his own report, made at the time of the break-in. The night-watchman had been knocked unconscious and tied up. The alarm system had been deactivated, which naturally caused suspicion to fall on the staff, but an impasse had been reached. He signed off and went to join the others for the morning's briefing.

Detective Chief Inspector Roper put it succinctly. 'We've reached a dead end. We still have no idea what happened to Charlie after 1820 hours when he left the off-licence. I've spoken to Martyn Bright – he's agreed to do a front-page piece in the *Herald* tomorrow, a "do you know this man" type of thing, but I'm not optimistic.' Even the prospect of defeat did nothing to detract from his imposing presence. Those who didn't know him might have guessed at some military training, but standing tall helped disguise the small paunch that was developing.

'Campbell, you continue with missing persons. Emmanuel, you chase up Social Security. I know.' He held up a restraining hand. 'But keep at it. If you get in their hair for long enough they'll make an effort.' He delegated someone else to chase up the dentists. 'Okay. That's it. Ask questions and make sure you listen to the answers.'

Thursday, like many other days before it, turned out to be frustrating. Ian got the feeling that valuable time was being wasted but could not think of a better way of deploying it. No luck with the DSS, no luck with the dentists. Where else could they look? If they knew who the man was they might learn who his friends and enemies were. 'Not even a bloody name,' he cursed again as he pulled his collar up against the chill wind. Darkness had descended early as rain clouds threatened. It seemed almost impossible that a man could get himself murdered without at least one person knowing exactly who he was.

'Or not saying,' he reminded himself as he got into his car.

A spattering of rain hit the windscreen. At least he was warm and dry, unlike those he passed waiting at bus stops. One or two cautious folk had had the forethought to carry umbrellas; the rest were huddled in groups trying to keep dry as best they could.

The traffic ground to a halt at the roundabout by the supermarket. Ian's temper began fraying at the edges and he cursed again, this time at the planners who designed the thing a year or two ago. The idea was to ease congestion. Since the day of its construction the hold-ups had been longer. It would have been more sensible to stay at work until after the rush hour.

The wipers flicked rhythmically with a soothing clunk each time they reached the horizontal position. Momentarily the rain stopped and the rubber blades squeaked in protest against the drying glass. The vehicles ahead inched forwards, their brake-lights shining every couple of feet. A barrage of hailstones hit the roof of the car, startling Ian. They melted on contact. Summer was no more than a memory now.

It was a relief to be home. He thought of the tramps as he closed the front door. He was surrounded by warmth and a meal would be waiting. Impossible to imagine living as they did.

Moira heard his key in the lock and came out to meet him. After a day like today it was a pleasure to see her. Fifteen years his junior, slim and attractive, she was the best medicine he could think of. She had completed a secretarial/business course the previous year, but finding a job had proved less easy than she had hoped. Optimistically she had pictured an office with deep pile carpet and a profusion of pot plants. Reality was a lot different. She settled for a firm of builders where the furniture looked ready for the junk yard. Most of what she had learned in the classroom was redundant, but it was a start and she found she enjoyed the work, and the hours suited. She spent her time between nine and one typing estimates, filing, answering the phone and making tea for anyone who happened to drop in. Some of the men would sit on the corner of her desk sipping their tea, smoking and chatting. She no longer blushed at the remarks they made.

Ian had to admit it was doing her good. Throughout their marriage she had remained at home looking after the house, himself and Mark. She had busied herself with committees and Ian had thought it was enough for her. It seemed it wasn't. It came as a bombshell when Moira told him she was bored. But his biggest fear did not materialise. He knew his attitude was unfair and unreasonable and totally selfish when he considered what she had put up with over the years, but he was very glad his home life was not disrupted in any way. She still managed to see to everything. She had surprised herself, discovering the more she had to do, the more quickly it got done.

Ian was hoping for a plate of stew and dumplings or liver and bacon with plenty of onions, but did not complain when the spaghetti bolognaise and a side salad were placed in front of him. Moira frequently cooked his favourites; this was one of hers.

'Mark's taken up tennis,' she said apropos of nothing.

'What?' Ian stopped eating. 'How can he?' He frowned at the kitchen window. Sleety rain was still slanting down.

'Honestly! Haven't you heard of indoor courts? He's at the leisure centre.'

'And who's paying for that?' Mark had pocket money but no Saturday job. A paper round was never a possibility – he struggled to get up in time for school.

'Me.'

Ian allowed this piece of information to sink in. Moira had told him what she earned but it hadn't sunk in. He had always made sure she had enough money and she had never wasted it. This new independence frightened him a little, but only because he enjoyed discussing all their financial decisions with her.

'Tennis,' he said, 'I don't understand it. He hates sport.'

'No, it's just football he doesn't like.'

Ian shook his head. He believed there was something seriously wrong with anyone who did not like the game.

'What's this all in aid of?'

'University. He knows if he's to get a place he needs more than chess and drama to put on his CV.'

This was not the first time Ian had been amazed at his son's forward planning. When he was Mark's age all he worried about was getting to Norwich away matches.

Mark returned at nine thirty, smiling but starving.

'Honestly,' Moira said later, 'to hear him talk you'd think he was getting ready for Wimbledon.'

All day Friday it poured with rain. The preliminary inquest was unnecessary. It was a formality, more for the purpose of identification and for the sake of the relatives. In this case there was neither.

The sky hung low and heavy with moisture and suited Ian's mood as he drove to work. He should be facing a pile of reports and statements. He knew he would not be.

Seated at his desk he made a chain of paperclips whilst he decided what his next move must be, and wondered how long it would be before he was told to ease up, to slacken the manpower because other, newer crimes needed attention. Thus occupied he did not see Judy Robbins until she spoke.

'You wanted to know,' she said.

'Debbie Wilkes?'

'Not Debbie Wilkes. It's more than likely her name is Amanda Philpotts. Known as Mandy. She went missing two years ago, when she was seventeen.'

'Local?'

'No. London. Seems she ran off with the boyfriend. They were believed to have been seen in Felixstowe about a year ago. No trace since.'

'What makes you think it's the same girl?'

'The description's close enough. Right age, and two distinguishing marks. Appendix scar and a small butterfly tattoo on her right shoulder. The hospital confirmed both. Apart from that her hair's not the same colour and

63

she's much thinner. Her parents have been contacted. If it is her, they want her to go home.'

'Not much we can do there. She's of age. Keep at it, Judy. Let's hope she hasn't gone far.'

'She's got to be getting the money for drugs from somewhere. I'll check with the DSS as well. If she's been here some time she's probably signed on.'

'They're just going to love us.'

'Pardon?'

'Nothing. Go on.'

By lunchtime Ian knew he needed some breathing space, if only for an hour.

'Doing anything important?' he asked DS Swan, who obviously wasn't because he was seated at a desk in the general office picking his teeth with a match.

'Trying to make some sense of all this. I'm not getting anywhere, though.'

'Well, get your coat. We're going to have a decent lunch.'

Barry struggled to keep up with Ian as they braved the High Street, walking directly into the driving rain.

'It's a long time since I've been in here,' he said, pushing open the door of Tandoori Delights. Pungent smells greeted them.

'Mr Roper, sir, nice to see you. A long time now since you come to see us.' The waiter took their wet coats and went to hang them up, indicating they could sit where they pleased. They chose a window seat, laid for four. It did not matter, they were the only customers. Most of the trade was done in the evening.

The waiter reappeared from the nether regions bearing two plastic menu cards. 'A drink on the house, gentlemen, as it's been such a long time?'

They both accepted. 'I'll stay away more often,' Ian commented as they decided what they wanted to eat.

They chose a main meal each and opted to share the rice and vegetables between them. 'And half a carafe of house red,' Ian added. 'Red all right with you?'

'Fine,' Barry replied. The Chief was certainly pushing the boat out.

The food, when it came, was good and they ate for some time in silence. When they'd almost finished Ian went to get the *Rickenham Herald* from his mac pocket.

'Bright's done quite a good job.' On the front page was a more than usually accurate sketch of Charlie, but the artist had had the actual subject to work from. There was no available photograph and one taken after his death was hardly tasteful. Brief details of the time and place were given, but not the cause. Underneath, the words 'Can you help?' were printed. There was a request for witnesses to come forward and the usual promise of confidentiality.

'Think we'll get any response?' Barry asked when he, too, had finished reading it.

'We can only keep our fingers crossed.' He signed the slip for the credit card which the waiter took to the till. 'Markham's got it into his head he might have known, or seen, something or someone connected with the JC Warehousing robbery. I think we might try working on that angle.'

'It's certainly a possibility. Here . . .' Barry got out his wallet.

'My treat. You can pay next time, when we get to meet your Lucy.'

'I see.' Barry should have known he wasn't going to be let off that lightly.

'Any messages?' the Chief asked when they got back.

'No, sir, nothing for you,' the desk sergeant replied, backing off slightly as the garlic fumes hit him.

Nor were there any relating to Operation Charlie for

65

the rest of the afternoon. Not one call came through in response to the article in the *Herald*. Operation Charlie was slowly grinding to a halt.

To top it all, when he arrived home Moira had gone to the trouble of making a steamed steak and kidney pudding but he was still too sated with his earlier meal to do it justice.

6

In the early hours of Saturday morning DCI Roper slept soundly, one arm flung across Moira, also asleep, the nocturnal activities of criminals temporarily unheeded.

DS Swan was also enjoying the respite of a good night's rest. In his case, Lucy's arm was around his waist as she lay curled into his back. Sometime during the course of the last few months he had come to the decision that this was the woman he wanted to marry. But he had not yet asked her.

The night patrol cars cruised around the town and the beat men walked the streets, routinely checking shop doors and generally keeping an eye on things so the citizens of the town could sleep in safety. They were not always successful, but they did the best they could.

Only after the drunks had been sent on their way or locked up for the night, when the late watering holes were closed and shuttered and domestic violence was taking a break until daylight, only then could these preservers of law and order snatch a few minutes for a cup of coffee or a fag. Then there was the long haul until dawn, or the end of the shift, depending on the seasons, and the return to the canteen for bacon and eggs and the satisfaction of watching the early shift arrive still bleary with sleep, and knowing their own beds were waiting.

William Golding felt the cold that night. The fire had

not been a success despite their efforts. The rain was too heavy, the wood too wet to keep it going enough to give off much heat.

He retired early and lay huddled under the shelter with all his clothes piled on top of him. He was surprised to hear the others snoring or tossing and turning. Perhaps it was just he who was cold. Perhaps it was time to call it a day. He thought back over his life and wondered at just what point it had all started to go wrong. He strongly suspected that his father was right, that no matter what he did there was no help for him. He was born bad. Things had recently come to a head. Too many things, one after the other.

'Oh, well,' he told himself philosophically before he finally slept, 'it had to happen sometime.'

There was one man who could not sleep and felt sure he never would again. He lay in his single bed desperate to shut out the world for a few hours. His brain would not let him.

How he had got through the day was beyond him, but he had filled it with all the small repairs that needed doing around the place. If only he could sleep, surely the answer would become clear in the morning. It might be that if he did nothing, nothing would happen. His conscience did not go along with that. Now he knew for certain, there were only two other options. It was a case of which to choose.

The triple-niner was connected at 2.30 a.m. on Saturday morning, but not to the police station. Within seconds an ambulance was on its way to Saxborough Road, unimpeded by traffic. It arrived only seven minutes after the call was placed.

Mandy Philpotts was made as comfortable as possible, put on a drip and taken to the Accident and Emergency Department at Rickenham General. She was in the theatre almost before the surgeon had finished scrubbing up. X-rays showed a broken rib pressing on her lung. Her other injuries were numerous but not life-threatening. The trauma consultant on duty suggested to the sister that, when she had a few minutes, she ought to inform the police because he was tired of patching up people deliberately injured by other people and because he could not help but see the needle tracks.

The second incident, which occurred almost simultaneously, was not reported until six thirty.

Geoffrey Simpson, duty sergeant for the morning, studied the list of night-time criminal activity. He sighed. Youngsters seemed to have lost any spark of imagination. Too much television, he reckoned. He could become quite boring on the subject. He did not believe that the joyriders who were arrested last night would have been quite so stupid if they had not seen their peers in other places behaving in such a way. It was common practice now everywhere. The telephone interrupted this line of thought.

'It can't have been,' he said rubbing his chin in disbelief, knowing it was a ridiculous thing to say, especially for a man in his position. He had fallen into the same trap as the general public, believing that victims of crime were always someone else, never yourself. In this instance it was not actually himself, but Rickenham Athletic Football Club where he was a social member and where he'd spent a pleasant couple of hours last night sipping a few drinks with his wife while they listened to a country and western band. They hadn't stayed late, not with an early shift the following day.

He took down the details and arranged for a car to be despatched.

Jim Knight, the steward of the social club bar, had reported the burglary. Mr Knight was questioned as to why he was on the premises at that time of day. 'I live out at Little Endesley,' he said, 'but my wife's away at her sister's, and, well, you know how it is. I've got a girlfriend. Her husband's having a hernia seen to, so, well, we made the most of the opportunity.' The interviewing officer did know. Some years ago he had told his wife he was working extra night duties. He was now ashamed of the fact, and therefore not as sympathetic towards Mr Knight as he might have been.

'We didn't want to upset anyone,' Knight continued. 'We've always agreed on that. So I left just after six so's no one would see me. I'd had a few drinks so I left the car round the back of the club and walked. That's how I came to see the damage.' The interviewing officer was tempted to breathalyse him if he was intending to drive home, but decided against it. Later his statement was verified by the lady in question, who prayed she would not be required to appear in court.

'And that's all that's missing?' The list consisted of only two items, apart from damage to the fruit machines which were emptied on Saturday nights and would quickly be replaced by the lessors. A case of vodka, which had been locked in the cleaning cupboard instead of being stored with the rest of the spirits behind the metal grilles of the bar, and the first team's kitbag, containing all their kit, were the two items.

'I can't understand it,' Jim Knight said. 'I mean, the kit's no use to anyone, and it's needed for this afternoon's match. They'll have to wear the change strip. I expect some damned official'll have something to say about that. It's the damage that bugs me, though. We've only just had the place done up.' The interviewing officer had seen a lot worse. It would take no more than a few hours to get things shipshape.

70

Jim Knight had been hoping to snatch a couple of hours' sleep before returning to the club to open up for the lunchtime session. Instead, he spent the morning on the telephone and clearing up.

'Not even a football club is inviolate these days,' the Chief commented when he heard about it, but he was more concerned with the news that Mandy Philpotts was once more within reach. He was going to get his teeth into this drugs business with or without the drugs squad. At the moment the situation did not warrant calling upon their services.

Judy Robbins was on duty and, as she was the most involved, she was sent to sit with Mandy Philpotts pending her recovering enough to talk.

'How is she now?' the Chief asked Barry.

'Round from the anaesthetic but sleeping. Her parents are on their way. Let's hope she makes it.'

'What're we doing about the other girls?'

'They've made statements, both of which tally. They share a flat, they'd all gone out separately and returned at different times. They claim they know nothing about drugs and that the first they knew of Mandy being in trouble was when they heard a scream. She was in the kitchen and whoever had done it had gone, leaving all the doors open.'

'Do you believe it?'

'Hard to say. If they'd had a few drinks they might have been sound asleep, but if what I've heard about her injuries is true, I'm sure there'd've been more than one scream.'

'So who are they protecting? And why?'

'Has to be, doesn't it? The dealer or the pusher. The house was clean, though. They even had a sniffer dog over there. Just because Mandy's a user, doesn't mean the other two are, but they must have known about her habit.'

'Seems as if they're scared the same might happen to them. It's a start. We'll follow it up.'

'I've already started. Marie O'Doyle and Sheila Dixon have no record.' Mandy Philpotts' credentials had already been checked. 'There's something, though, which isn't quite right.'

'Which is?'

'None of them have bona fide jobs. They all take casual work, including Mandy, and none of them are claiming benefits. And they've lived there for over a year.'

'I see what you're getting at. A reasonable address but no recorded regular income.'

'Exactly.'

'On the game?'

'It crossed my mind. Want me to see them myself?'

'I'm sure you'd love that, Swan, but no, not just for the moment. Come on, breakfast calls. It's an ungodly hour to be at work.'

Whilst Barry and Ian sat in the canteen with tea and toast, a more than conscientious uniformed sergeant was compiling a list. He was sick to death of unsolved minor crimes, especially breaking and entering where the cost of repairing the damage to property far outweighed the value of the goods taken. The football club was the last straw. In the list he included the name of every thief, every petty villain, every greedy little bastard he'd ever had the misfortune of coming across. And he was going to find out where they all were between the time Jim Knight locked up and his return in the morning.

He had to tread very softly; there must not be even a whisper of police harassment. He picked his men carefully and with good reason. The whole operation was to be very casual, very informal.

It was PCs Jackson and Stone who, later that day, on

the last of their backshifts, had the dubious pleasure of calling upon the Tuckers. Frank Stone, the elder of the two by some twenty years, had known Maureen Tucker since their schooldays. He knew the family history inside out but remained on friendly terms with her. She would not close the door in his face. Hence the reason they were sent.

'Oh, God, not again,' she said resignedly when she opened the front door. 'Come on in. What've they been up to this time?' Her exasperation was with her family, not her visitors. Her husband was on the dole, claiming he couldn't work because of ill health. Long ago he had given up any pretence of interest in his family and spent his time watching television or going to the betting shop. Her sons, Terry and Peter, were also unemployed. That is, they drew unemployment benefit, which is not quite the same thing.

Frank Stone gave Maureen the once-over, his eyes travelling the length of her body. She had always been a looker and despite her problems kept her home and herself nice. She was slim but full-breasted and dressed a bit on the tarty side but managed to get away with it. She was proud of her assets. Her raunchiness appealed to Frank's baser side although he'd never done anything about it.

'Want a cuppa?' she asked. 'I was just about to make one for that lazy bugger in there.' She thumbed towards the closed sitting-room door. If Mr Tucker had seen them arrive he showed no sign of it.

'No, thanks all the same,' PC Jackson answered quickly, seeing by his partner's face how the land lay. 'It's your boys we want to talk to.'

Maureen arched an eyebrow. 'Pity,' she said, her expression causing him to blush. 'We could've had a little chat.' They followed her out to the kitchen and waited while she filled the kettle.

'Burglary, I suppose?'

'The football club.'

'I didn't think Terry went down there any more.'

'Oh?' PC Stone forced his eyes away from the two semicircles of flesh showing above the frill of her cerise blouse.

'Not since he couldn't get a place in the team. Pete used to train down there once, but he wasn't ever any good. Terry was, but they kept putting him in the reserve side. He got fed up and told them what they could do.'

'How long ago was this, Maureen?' Here, Frank Stone thought, was a very good reason for dumping the first team kit.

'I'm not sure. Not all that long.'

'Are they in?'

'Pete is. Terry's . . . out.' She stopped herelf in time from saying working.

'Call him for us, love, will you?'

She did so. Pete joined them in the kitchen, his face sullen.

He'd been at his girlfriend's place all night, he said. They could check. They said they would.

'Where was your brother?'

'How should I know?'

Maureen did not know either. 'I didn't hear him come in but it must've been late because I didn't go up myself until nearly one. He was down for breakfast this morning and his bed was slept in.'

She did not take the trouble to lie for her sons; there was no point. They were so inept as criminals they always got caught.

'Do you think we could have a look in his room?'

'Got a warrant?' Pete interrupted.

'Leave it, Pete. It's all right,' his mother said. 'You carry on. If he's got nothing to hide it won't matter.' Or it might be one less mouth to feed if he spent a couple of months inside. But Terry would not be stupid enough to bring stuff into the house.

But it seemed he was.

'The daft little sod,' Maureen exclaimed when she saw the carton of vodka they retrieved from under a pile of clothes in his wardrobe, 'and I always thought he was the clever one.' Pete Tucker looked suitably hurt.

The search was worthwhile. They also found a video recorder and some jewellery.

Maureen confirmed she hadn't seen these things before and she doubted very much if they were her son's property.

'We'll have to take them with us.'

She saw them out, mulling over what heinous thing she'd done in a past life to deserve a family such as this in her present one. She had no option but to tell them where they might find Terry. He was doing some roofing on the side. They went to pick him up.

DS Swan took the chair on the opposite side of the table in the interview room and offered his packet of cigarettes. 'All right, Terry, let's hear it.'

Terry grinned and took a cigarette. 'Cheers, mate.' He was a small-time thief, never violent, and was, despite his part-time trade, extremely likeable. When Jackson and Stone arrived outside the house on whose roof he was working he had given a wave and climbed down the ladders. He didn't deny anything.

'No. No point in dragging a brief out on a Saturday afternoon,' he said, when he was asked if he wanted a solicitor. 'He won't be able to do much for me anyway.'

'Just the three premises, is it? The two flats and the football club? Why on earth do you do it, Terry? You know you always get caught.'

'Can't seem to help myself. Mind you, the club was

different. Couldn't run a piss-up in a brewery. Everyone except the manager knew I was good enough for the first team. They wouldn't be in the position they're in now if I'd been there to score a few goals. Serves them right.' He grinned again. 'I chucked the kit in the stream, under the bridge.'

'All right. It all adds up. Except the video recorder. Now, where did you get it?'

'Come on, Serge, you know me by now. I've told you everything. It came from one of the flats.' But Barry was recalling what PC Stone said after they'd brought Terry in. About his feelings that the man Miller was hiding something, that he suspected he might have had a video which, for some reason, he did not wish to report missing. Terry was probably telling the truth. Once he was in the nick he usually did. Barry left him in the hands of a PC and went to report to the Chief and Markham, who would certainly be interested.

'Alan Campbell's running it through,' Barry said, hanging his maroon wool jacket on the door. 'Checking the serial number. Shouldn't take long. If it is from JC Warehousing where are the rest of them, and how come we haven't heard of them being offered on the streets?'

'We'll have to wait and see.' He hoped it was the case. Just one small lead and Markham would be on to it like a dog with a bone.

The telephone rang. The Chief grunted once or twice, said thank you and replaced the receiver.

'Philpotts' parents have arrived at the hospital. I'm going to see them myself. Take over for a while, will you? And get Campbell to do me a list of the big-time boys, both for theft and drugs, those that aren't banged up at the moment.' Enigmatically he left it at that.

7

The serial number of the video corresponded to one of the stolen ones. Markham set off to interview George Miller. He took the car. He had a strong suspicion he would be bringing the man down to the station to make a statement.

The Chief set off in the opposite direction, towards the hospital, which was an enormous building on the out-skirts of the town. It had replaced Redlands Hospital and the old cottage hospital which were now used for outpatients' clinics and geriatric wards.

He drove around the car-park until he found a space as near the main entrance as possible. There, he followed the signs for the intensive care unit.

'She's asleep. We've put her on quite high doses of pain-killers. I don't think you'll have much luck if you're here to question her,' the sister in charge told him after he'd shown her his identity.

'It's okay. It's her parents I'm more interested in at the moment. Would you happen to know where they are?'

'I've sent them down to the cafeteria. It's been a long day for them. They came up by train.' They exchanged a sympathetic smile. It was easy enough to get from London to Ipswich but after that there were two changes and usually a long wait in between. 'Mrs Philpotts is wearing a black and white tweed coat and a black knitted hat, if it's any help to you.'

'Thanks. I'll find them.' He turned to WPC Robbins, who was sitting on a plastic chair flicking through the pages of a magazine one of the nurses had found for her. She shook her head. 'She hasn't opened her eyes. Not a word out of her. Do I stay? Now that her parents are here?'

'Yes. I'll send someone up to relieve you later.'

He asked directions to the cafeteria and was surprised to notice that it offered hot meals as well as drinks and sandwiches. He recalled the opening of the hospital by a member of the royal family just over three years ago and the amount of work and manpower necessary to ensure the security of the visit.

Even without the sister's description, the Chief felt he might have recognised Mrs Philpotts. She was short and dumpy with rosy, well-rounded cheeks. It was a face meant for smiling, pleasant and motherly. Now her expression was a combination of disbelief, hope and anxiety.

'Mr and Mrs Philpotts?'

The couple looked up. Mr Philpotts, thin and balding and dressed in his only suit, held his wife's hand across the table, cups of tea cooling in front of them. Mr Philpotts nodded.

'I'm Chief Inspector Roper, CID. How do you do?' He held out a hand. They each limply shook it in turn. 'Before I say any more, can I get you another cup of tea?'

It seemed they were incapable of coming to that simple decision, so he went quickly to the counter and came back with a tray bearing three more cups.

'Thank you,' Mrs Philpotts said, her eyes filling with tears, 'you're very kind. I can't believe it. What sort of trouble is she in? It's just, well . . .' but she couldn't continue.

'You see, sir, Mr Philpotts interrupted, 'my wife and I had given up hope. After a year, when she couldn't be found, we tried to convince ourselves she was dead. It seemed the only thing to do at the time. Day after day, waiting for a knock at the door or the telephone to ring, it just got too much. We tried so hard to put her out of our minds, but it wasn't any use.' He paused. 'And then this. It makes me feel so ashamed to think she was alive all the time.'

'You mustn't look at it that way. Mandy had every opportunity to contact you.' It was a brutal statement to make to two people in such distress but it was better to be honest.

'Yes.' Mr Philpotts drained his cup.

'I hardly recognised her,' his wife said. 'She's gone so very thin, and her hair . . . Oh, it's all right, it's definitely Mandy.'

'I realise you're both upset, but would you mind if I ask you a few questions? Here, or somewhere more private if you prefer.'

'Here will do.'

'Can you describe Mandy to me, what sort of girl she was, who her friends were, that sort of thing?'

'It's two years. Then her friends were people from school. She was doing well, too, until she got mixed up with Danny.'

'Danny?'

'Danny Grant. Her boyfriend. We knew they were seeing each other, we weren't keen, Marge and I, but we thought we knew better than to try to stop her. Then one day she went off to school as usual and never came home. She got a girlfriend to ring us up and tell us.'

'Not a pleasant way of breaking the news, Mr Philpotts. It must've been a bad time for you. Did you have any reason to think she might have been taking drugs?'

Mrs Philpotts looked him straight in the eye. 'I wasn't

certain. I don't know what you must think of me, Chief Inspector, but Mandy was going through an awkward stage at the time – you know how teenagers can be?' The Chief did know. 'I was waiting for the right time to tackle her. It never came. I'm sorry, Dave,' she said to her husband. 'I know I should've told you. I thought I could sort it out myself. If there was a problem, that is. She is, isn't she? On drugs? That's why she looks so awful.'

'Yes, Mrs Philpotts, she is. But they'll start weaning her off them here. The rest, as you know, is up to her. My interest is in where she gets them.'

'I don't know. I suspected Danny but there was nothing to prove it.'

'Do you know where Danny is?'

'No. As I said, they left together.'

'Would you happen to have his last address?'

'No, but he came from Lewisham.'

'How old is this Danny?'

'He's a couple of years older than Mandy, twenty-two or three. I'm not sure.' Then, the Chief thought, they might be able to find out where he was last known. He would have been over eighteen at the time of his disappearance and was hopefully on the Register of Electors at the relevant time. 'I know he was living with his parents. Mandy told me they wanted him to find a place of his own.'

Even better. It was possible the senior Grants were still in residence. 'Were there any problems before, apart from the usual teenage ones?'

'Before she met Danny? No. She was just an ordinary girl, into clothes and records and spending hours on the telephone with her friends. What sort of friends does she have now, to get herself beaten up like this?'

'That's what we're trying to find out. I think we can leave it at that for the moment. Thank you both for your time. I expect you want to get back to your daughter now.'

All three stood. The Philpotts went left, towards the lift; the Chief went out to the car-park. Many more spaces were filled now, because of the less rigid visiting system. Anxious relatives hurried across the tarmac, pulling on coats and macs to combat the unending rain. His next task was to find Danny Grant.

David Victor Marsh knew he could pull any girl he wanted. Enough of them had told him how good-looking he was. Their opinion was confirmed each time he saw his reflection in a mirror, and he did that a lot. Chin up, shoulders back, it was also pleasing to catch a glimpse of himself in shop windows. His legs were long and muscled, his stomach flat and his shoulders wide. He did not follow the current fashion but kept his pale, almost white, hair cut short at the sides with a smooth lock which fell forward and rested on one eyebrow. Girls always reached out to push it back. In his left ear he wore a small gold cross on a sleeper.

Today, dressed in jeans, white T-shirt and brown leather jacket, clothes he knew flattered his figure further, he set off in his Y-registered Sierra in the direction of Felixstowe where he was to meet Danny Grant.

He had known Danny in London and only Danny knew his first name was David. David, or worse, Dave, was too common. He was known as Vic.

Markham drove through the streets of terraced housing, respectability etched in every brick. Net curtains were pristine, gardens were neat. There were no spilling sacks of rubbish, no cars or bikes half taken apart and no noise carrying into the street. What went on behind those nets might be a different matter, but outwardly everything in the garden was rosy. These homes were mortgaged, many of the occupants having managed to leave behind accommodation and circumstances like those that existed two streets away, where Markham was heading.

The flats, which were actually called Magnolia House, were in Waveney Road. The same council that built them fixed a theme for the necessary new roads, naming them after Suffolk rivers. Not many of the residents were aware of that fact, or if they were, they didn't care. And right from the start Magnolia House had simply been called 'the flats'.

George Miller was at home. His bloodshot eye leered at Markham through the spyhole.

'Police,' he said.

Miller opened the door the length of the security chain he'd fitted that morning.

'Let's see your identity.' He could usually spot the Old Bill a mile off. Something about Markham left him in doubt.

Markham produced it and held it in a position whereby Miller could see without having to relinquish his hold.

The door shut briefly while the chain was removed then opened wider.

'George Miller?' Markham already had his foot in the door. The squalor did not disgust him. People were what disgusted him; his own lack of control occasionally disgusted him. He worked out at a gym twice a week, he usually ate well and mostly he kept his drinking within moderation. It was only when he was particularly lonely that he went on a bender. He could not discover what it was within himself which prevented him forming close relationships.

'Yeah. I'm Miller.'

'I believe you were the victim of a robbery on Wednesday evening.'

Miller, mistaking the reason for the visit, smiled. 'You've found my things? My radio? Kids, I suppose. It usually is.'

There were several ways in which Markham could have dealt with these questions. Naturally, he chose the most unorthodox.

'We have found your video.'

Miller's grin disappeared and his unhealthy skin turned a different shade of grey. 'I don't have no video. I never reported one missing, did I?' A nervous line of spittle played out from his mouth to the tip of the cigarette he removed from it as he denied ownership.

'Odd that,' Markham commented casually, 'because it's got your fingerprints all over it.'

'Oh, shit!' Miller sank into the only armchair in the room, his head resting against its greasy back. 'I didn't nick it, honestly. Hang on, wait a minute . . .' but it was too late. He'd fallen for one of the oldest tricks in the book. They could not know they were his prints, he'd never had them taken.

Markham smiled. It was not a reassuring sight. Miller sank further into his chair.

'If you didn't nick it, who did? You certainly didn't buy it in Dixon's.'

'I got it from a man in a pub.'

'Oh, really? From a man in a pub.' Markham moved closer. 'Listen, you disgusting old sod, I want to know which man and which pub. And I want to know now.'

'The Prince William.'

The answer took Markham by surprise. How come he didn't know about it? That was the last time his informer was receiving any money from him. But the rest of the recorders? It still didn't add up.

'And the man's name?'

'I don't know. I swear it.' At least Markham was spared the 'on my mother's grave' bit. 'I just happened to be there when they came in.'

'I see. You were sitting there minding your own business when a total stranger comes up to you and asks if you want to buy a knocked-off video?'

'No. I was at the next table. I overheard them talking, see. It was me that mentioned I might be interested.'

'How interested?'

'What?'

'How much did you pay for it?' Miller told him. The recession must be hitting harder than he imagined if the things were going so cheaply. 'And I can take it you didn't pay by cheque.' Miller ignored the intended sarcasm. 'Is he local, the man?'

'I've seen one of them before but not the other.'

'Okay. Get your coat on, Miller, we're going for a little drive.'

Miller knew he was beaten. He also knew they wouldn't do much to an old man with no record for such a minor offence. He would not be able to lie successfully, not to this man. Best to get it over with. Together they went down to the car.

'Wait there,' Markham said when they reached the next floor down. He knocked on Mrs Bennet's door, showing her his identity when she answered without being asked for it.

'We've recovered your bits of jewellery,' he told her. 'We'll let you know when you can collect them.'

'Oh, thank you,' she said, her eyes filling with tears. 'It's not worth much but the brooch was a present from my son. He saved up for it with his pocket money when he was little. And a ring my husband gave me. I can't wear it now,' she held up a hand, the joints swollen with arthritis. 'I can't thank you enough, young man.'

'That's all right. Part of the job.' For one horrifying

moment he thought she was going to kiss him. He left quickly, nodding at Miller to follow him.

'He admits it, yes,' Markham told the Chief. 'He says there were two men, one local, one probably not. He also said he didn't think he was the type of bloke to use somewhere like the Prince William. Too smartly dressed.'

'Find out who they are, Markham. Get them and we might have a very happy warehouse owner. Lean on Miller a bit if you have to, but not too hard. He's not young and he's obviously very frightened.'

The Chief watched him leave, shoulders untypically hunched. He'd give a week's salary to know what went on in his head.

Vic Marsh's meeting with Danny Grant went well. They made the deal and parted, never staying together a second longer than was necessary. It would be another ten, or maybe more, days before they met again. That was all right – as long as Danny kept to his side of the bargain. Vic had a feeling he was tiring of it. He laughed. Danny was trapped. Without Vic's say-so, there was no way out.

Saturday drew to a close. Mandy Philpotts' condition remained stable. Perhaps tomorrow they would be able to get a statement.

As for Operation Charlie, the HOLMES computer might as well have not existed. It needed to be fed information in order to make links; it needed background information. They were still without the victim's name.

Before going home Barry and Ian decided to go back

to the old method. They made a list. The possible suspects were the other vagrants, despite the uselessness of their statements, the woman who served him in the off-licence, but only because she was the last person known to have seen him alive . . . 'And?' Ian said.

'And that's it.'

'Wonderful.' Ian moved across towards the window and stared at the stream of cars passing by below him.

'This woman, Helen Winters, isn't it? I can't really see her knocking him off.'

'Nor me. Her record at the shop's exemplary. If she'd fallen upon hard times and seen Charlie had money, and if Charlie'd been robbed, maybe. But even then it would be easier to fiddle the till.'

'Shall I cross her off?'

'Yes.'

'Not much of a list, is it?'

Ian returned to his desk and shuffled through some papers. Several clear sets of prints had been lifted from the whisky bottle. Charlie's and Helen Winters' could be explained. The rest might belong to anyone from the bottling plant to the distillery to the warehouse. How neat if one could be matched to someone already on their files.

How impossibly optimistic.

There were mixed feelings amongst the men; relief at the lead concerning JC Warehousing and a sense of dread that the riddle of Charlie's murder would never be solved.

'Operation Bugger All, if you ask me,' one of them said after the evening's debriefing.

'Come on, you know how it goes,' DC Winston Emmanuel replied. 'Elimination, etc., etc.'

'Oh, really? I don't think I've heard that one. And just tell me who we've eliminated?'

'No need for tantrums. Anyone for a drink?'

Barry said that as Lucy was at her parents' place in Wickham Market for the night, he, for one, would go. Several others agreed. 'Only if it's the Crown,' the Chief added. 'And I won't be staying long.'

'You and your Adnams,' Winston sighed. 'Now, to my way of thinking, there's nothing like a drop of pale rum.'

They straggled up the road towards the Crown.

'At least we haven't got Ross breathing down our necks,' Barry commented.

'True,' Ian said. At least with Superintendent Thorne, when he asked you to head up an inquiry he meant just that and left you to get on with it. All he required were regular progress reports.

'Why do we do it? This job?' Barry said to no one in particular.

'It's in the blood,' Winston chipped in. 'Once a cop, always a cop.'

'Talking about blood,' DC Alan Campbell said, 'I don't know what courses through your veins, but I wish I had some of it. It surely works with the women.'

With this totally uncharacteristic comment the assembled company were stunned into silence. Alan Campbell sipped his lager, aware that his face was hot.

Moira had had a bath and was in her peach quilted dressing-gown and slippers when Ian returned. Her book lay open on the settee, face down, pages splayed. Ian bit his tongue. He might have irritating habits, but she had a couple of her own. This was one of them and had been the cause of the start of more than one argument over the years. He said nothing but picked it up and closed it, placing it on the sideboard with more noise than was necessary.

Moira, in the process of pouring herself a glass of wine, made a face behind his back. 'Bad day?' she asked sweetly.

'Bloody useless.'

She gave him ten minutes with the paper then tried again. Gradually he became more approachable. 'By the way, we've been invited out to dinner. Barry wants us to meet Lucy.'

'So you said. It sounds serious.'

'It is. I think he's ready to settle down.'

'You didn't until you were quite ancient.'

'What does that make me now?'

'You'll do. It's going badly at work then, is it?'

'It's not that – well, only partly. It's seeing a young girl's life ruined by drugs. It frightens me, what the future holds for the next generation.'

Moira was not in a mood to be sympathetic. 'Well, if it's any comfort, our contribution to the next generation is at the cinema with a girlfriend.'

Ian groaned. The last thing he needed was a reminder of the passing years. 'I hope he doesn't intend staying out until the small hours.'

'Ian, he's seventeen. And it's not his first girlfriend. She's very nice.'

'You've met her?' It seemed he was always the last person to know what was going on on the domestic front.

'Yes. The other afternoon. I'm sure I told you.'

She might have done. At work, he not only listened to what people had to say, he remembered it in almost every detail. The trouble was, when he walked through the door of 14 Belmont Terrace the same could not be said.

Mark came in at eleven thirty and went straight to his room, shouting good-night through the closed living-room door. Moira wondered if this was because he was afraid they would detect alcohol on his breath. She knew he had the odd pint but it was not something she was going to point out to Ian. The man in question said he was shattered and going to bed. 'I don't suppose I'll sleep, though, my brain's going round in circles.'

Fifteen minutes later, when Moira pushed open the bedroom door, the light was out and she could hear gentle snoring.

'Well, really, Chief Inspector,' she muttered, 'it *is* Saturday night.'

8

Since Superintendent Ross's departure Doc Harris no longer had to go through the pretence of taking his golf seriously. He was quietly sorry for the man. His dismissal was natural under the circumstances and he felt no sympathy for him on that score, but Ross's own embarrassment meant his resignation from several clubs including this one, the Elms Golf and Country Club. However, there were plenty of other willing partners whose company the Doc enjoyed. Often he had ended up partnered with Ross only because no one else liked him.

The Doc was a mediocre golfer who could occasionally astonish with a dazzling shot, but such was his personality that even players with decent handicaps were pleased to have him make up a four. It was really for the company of these other men, men unconnected with his surgery or police work or death, that he spent Sunday mornings, rain or shine, knocking a ball down the fairway. He also convinced himself it was doing him good, helping to counteract the two packets of cigarettes he consumed each day, his penchant for what he termed family-sized whiskies and Shirley's cooking.

Pleasantly rounded, he appeared far from intimidating. To their cost, people had underestimated his intellectual powers and his amazing insight. He knew so often when a patient's ailment was only the reaction to or escape from another sort of problem.

The fresh air was exactly that. A strong wind whipped abruptly across the course and if it had not been for the waterproofs they were wearing the Doc and his companions would have been soaked to the skin.

'Why do we leave our nice warm beds for this?' his partner asked, not requiring an answer. It was a question they often asked each other.

'It's your shot, Christopher.' This was the second time the Doc had had to remind one of the opposition.

'Sorry.' Christopher Chambers approached the ball, swung his club almost recklessly and sliced the ball off to the left of the fairway where it landed in the rough.

Later, in an attempt to draw the man out, the Doc asked, 'How's Madelaine?'

'Madelaine? Why?'

'Sorry, old chap. Tell me to mind my own business.'

'No. I'm sorry. I didn't mean to be rude. It's just that I've got a lot on my mind. I honestly don't even know what I'm doing here. I should never've come. I thought being outdoors would help me to think, but what I really should've done . . .'

Whatever it was, the Doc did not get to hear. A deluge of rain drove them to shelter under some trees where they debated whether it was worth going on.

'The bar doesn't open until twelve,' Doc Harris pointed out. 'We might as well give it a few minutes then risk another hole or two.'

This was agreed upon and by midday their dripping waterproofs were hanging in the locker room, their clubs and trolleys were stowed in the boots of their cars and they were seated on stools in the warmth of the bar.

Doc Harris lit the first cigarette of the day which did not disintegrate into a soggy mess. 'First one's on me,' he said.

They ordered their drinks while the barman, who didn't need to be told, held the Doc's favourite stubby tumbler twice under the optic. Two of the foursome left after one drink as they and their respective wives were sharing Sunday lunch.

'It shouldn't be allowed,' the Doc pointed out. 'Golf followed by a good session at the nineteenth should never be interfered with.'

Chambers managed a weak smile. 'Madelaine's never expected me home until I'm ready, I'll say that for her.'

'Quite right. Shirley would have a fit. She'd think something was seriously wrong if I got back before closing. Anyway, she likes Sunday mornings to potter around. Christopher, for the second time, tell me again to mind my own business, but what's troubling you?' Christopher was gazing at the rows of gleaming bottles behind the bar. 'And don't say nothing – I can see something is.' The Doc sipped his drink, hoping he hadn't gone too far. He hardly knew Chambers, after all.

'Oh, God. Is it that obvious? I just don't think I can go on. I'll have to do something about it. I'm sorry, Doc, I can't tell you. I'm not sure I can tell anyone. Thanks for the drink, but I'm afraid I've got to go.'

Doc Harris continued to sip his whisky until the glass was empty then ordered another. He speculated about what he knew of the Chambers' marriage. It had never been trouble-free. It was second time around for both of them and it was Madelaine who held the purse strings, having been left more than well off after the death of her first husband. At the time everyone agreed it could lead to problems.

It was also rumoured that, beautiful though Madelaine was, she was cold. Had Christopher, then, found another woman to provide the missing warmth? It seemed the most likely explanation.

He put it out of his mind and concentrated on raising his blood alcohol to the required level as more wet-headed players entered the bar. Shirley was bound to tut when he rang to ask her to collect him. She always did, but she always obliged. She could run him up to collect the car in the morning.

The breakthrough, when it came, was neither dramatic nor, initially, apparent, but it did start a chain reaction which led to solving both halves of the case.

It was the prominence of Martyn Bright's layout which did it. Had there been fisticuffs at a council meeting at the Town Hall, which always made the front page, Basil Wainright would not have come forward because he never read the *Rickenham Herald*.

His wife bought it religiously. Basil read the heavies. On Sunday morning, because it was too wet to perform the task outside, he placed the *Herald* on the draining board prior to cleaning his two pairs of working shoes. They were both black and identical and he wore them on alternate days.

Basil Wainright was known to be an upstanding citizen. Routine and respectability were the gods he worshipped. At least outwardly. Had his life not been ruled by the clock he might have waited until Sunday afternoon when the rain eased to clean his shoes, and he would not have seen Charlie's picture on the front page.

Routine for once out of the window, he took himself off to the police station. It was the first time he'd set foot in the place. 'I wish to speak to whoever's in charge of Operation Charlie,' he said, unaware that a telephone call would have brought someone to his door. 'I wish to speak with Detective Chief Inspector Roper or Detective Sergeant Swan, please.'

Sergeant Whitelaw, back on desk duty, raised his head and wondered if it really was Sunday. The man facing him wore an immaculate raincoat beneath which were sharply creased slacks, a white shirt and tie and a blazer.

His use of full titles revealed much about his personality. Had Sergeant Whitelaw been at home on a Sunday he would have been slopping around in comfortable cords, an old pullover and his slippers, and he certainly wouldn't have shaved, not unless the in-laws were coming for dinner. But then, he thought philosophically, it's as well we're not all the same or I'd be out of a job. The tang of aftershave prickled his nostrils as Wainright leaned an elbow on the desk.

'And you are, sir?'

'My name is Basil Wainright.'

Whitelaw wrote it down. 'And the nature of your business?'

'I have already said, I wish to see . . .'

'So you did, sir, but I need to know what about.'

'I should have thought it was obvious.'

'To you, sir, maybe, but not to me. We get all sorts in here.' Wainright blinked, unsure of the exact meaning of those last words. 'You see, the Chief Inspector and Sergeant Swan are very busy men. It's part of my job to see their time isn't wasted. Sometimes it's possible that someone of lesser rank can be of assistance.'

'No, they can't. I'm here about the murder of that poor man. It states quite clearly in the paper who to contact.'

Whitelaw did not point out that it also stated quite clearly the telephone number to ring. 'In that case, if you'd like to take a seat, I'll tell them you're here.'

Wainright did not like. He glanced at the chairs and, although they were modern and appeared fairly comfortable, he didn't like to think who had sat in them before.

'Someone'll be down in a minute,' Whitelaw said as he replaced the receiver.

Barry Swan came down the stairs two at a time. This was their first lead, possibly even a witness, after six days. It was too good to be true.

'DCI Roper's busy at the moment. I'm Detective

Sergeant Swan.' He showed Wainright into an interview room. 'Please have a seat.' Barry took the other chair and pulled a notepad towards him. His pen was already uncapped and in his hand.

'A few formalities first, Mr Wainright.'

He supplied his name and address and said he had read the article in the *Herald*.

'Only by chance, you understand. I just happened to see it this morning.'

The window behind Barry was pushed up about a foot. Despite the rain and the chilly draught which rattled the slatted blind over it, he left it open. Wainright's aftershave was overpowering. Barry watched him carefully. Although he was relaxed and easy whilst he gave his own details, Barry wondered how he would react to questioning. He was able to spot the signs of nervousness, of inner turmoil and fear. He was not as adept as the Chief but he was improving.

His first impression was that Wainright was homosexual. He pushed it firmly to the back of his mind. The man's slightly effeminate mannerisms and immaculate clothes suggested it but only in a stereotypical way. He'd known some very tough characters who were that way inclined.

'It may mean nothing,' Wainright began. Barry waited. All detectives knew how often what followed would prove to be the antithesis of those words. 'I saw this man, last Monday.' He held a copy of the *Rickenham Herald*, neatly folded to show Charlie's picture. 'He was outside my office, I mean the office where I work. It was just after six. I've seen him there before, but on Monday he was talking to someone.'

'Mr Wainright, it's very good of you to come forward like this, I only wish more people would do so, but it does actually say further on in the article that several other people also saw him. A few of them handed him money – it was probably one of these people you saw. I take it you're referring to the area of St Hilda's Walk?'

'Yes.'

'He was later seen alive elsewhere. We've already interviewed many of the office workers. How come you didn't speak up on Wednesday?'

'Wednesday? I'm sorry, I don't understand.' But Wainright was wringing his hands, no longer at ease.

'When our officers were interviewing people.'

'Oh, I see.' His relief was almost tangible. 'I was away. I went to Brussels on Tuesday and didn't return until late Friday night. I was due back on Thursday but was talked into staying an extra night. The job's all meetings and formal dinners when I'm in Europe. I couldn't resist a bit of relaxation.' And why, Barry wondered, can't he resist telling me all this? 'I can give you the number of my hotel if you wish.'

'Why should I need that, Mr Wainright?' Wainright didn't seem to know. 'You say you were not aware of this incident until you read about it this morning in the *Herald*?'

'That's right. I don't usually read it. My wife takes it and tells me anything of importance.'

'But not this time when there's a murder on your doorstep?'

Wainright looked at his hands, seeming surprised they were clasped tightly together. 'No. She wasn't very happy about me staying the extra night. She, well, we've hardly spoken since I got back.' Wainright was still on the defensive but interview rooms were not designed to put people at their ease. Barry believed the latter part of what the man said, the rest he was unsure of.

'Tell me anyway, the man you saw talking to the deceased, did you know him?'

'No, but I can describe him. Tall, greyish hair, smartly dressed. I assumed he worked in one of the offices.'

'Can you describe him in any more detail? A lot of men would look like that. Was he clean-shaven, for instance?'

'No, I don't think so. There was nothing about him which caught the eye.'

'Then what caught yours, Mr Wainright?'

'The incongruity, I suppose, in the two men. It was more than just handing him money, I'm sure of that. They were in deep conversation, then the smarter man handed the vagrant something.'

'Could they have been shaking hands, maybe?'

Wainright thought about it. 'No. I don't know how I know, but I do. He definitely handed him something.'

'Anything else?'

'No. It's just that the old boy didn't usually say much. He just muttered and walked off once he'd got a few shillings.'

'Are you saying they left together?'

Wainright shook his head. 'One went towards the car-park, the other towards the main road.'

'All right. I think, if you don't mind, I'd like to take a proper statement from you. Hopefully it won't take long.' There might be something in what Wainright said; it was worth a try in case something further came out.

Minutes after this was done the Chief appeared. 'Give me a fag, for God's sake. What a waste of time. What on earth do they get out of it?'

'I take it the information was incorrect?'

'Oh, very droll. Don't look so smug. All right, he got me going there for a while, he was so damn plausible. It was fifteen minutes before he started talking about being controlled by men from outer space. Oh, wipe that grin off your face, you didn't have to sit there and listen to it.'

'Fair enough. Still, he's been the only one in almost a week. By now we've usually had dozens of crackpots.

97

Now, I've just interviewed one Basil Wainright, who may not be all he appears. Claims he's only just read the *Herald* and that he saw Charlie in deep conversation with a suited gentleman on Monday night.'

'And?'

'And he's sure he saw this man give Charlie something.'

'A few coins, I expect.'

'He says not.'

'Did he seem genuine?' Having been duped himself, he half hoped the same had happened to Barry.

'Yes. I got a statement too. He was a bit touchy when he mentioned being abroad on business.'

'Abroad! Drugs?'

'Don't think he's got the nerve. You never know, though. Shall I make a few discreet inquiries?'

'No harm in doing so. That car-park. You need a pass to use it don't you?'

'I believe so. That should narrow it down a bit.'

'Hm.' The Chief took a packet of cigarettes from his shirt pocket and glanced at the contents to see how many were left. He offered one to Barry. 'What makes you say that?'

'Seems logical. Businessman finishes work, goes to get his car.'

'Don't bet on it.'

Barry's face dropped as his superior proceeded to do what he was so good at. He demolished Barry's theory.

'One,' he said, when his cigarette was alight, 'he only walked towards the car-park, he may not have entered it. Two, he might have simply gone there to get a lift home with someone. Three, he might not be a regular there, perhaps he just called on business. Four,' he was awkwardly ticking off the points on the fingers of one hand, hampered by the cigarette in the other. 'Four, he was using the car-park as a short cut. And five,' Barry's

98

face became gloomier with every number, 'and most important of all, nothing out of the ordinary took place. Wainright is either mistaken or a liar.'

'Damn it all, Ian. Just because you've been seen off by a crank.'

'We have to consider all the possibilities, although why the man should lie is beyond me. Perhaps he needs his own alibi for that particular time.'

Barry was defeated. How many times had the Chief told him always to assume a witness was lying until it was proved otherwise? 'Ah, well, you might be right. He admitted he spent an extra night away from home. Perhaps he was with someone he shouldn't have been and wants to convince his wife otherwise.'

Ian grinned and rested a hand on Barry's shoulder. The conciliatory gesture was wasted when a quarter of an inch of ash fell down the front of Barry's jacket. He brushed it off impatiently.

'But,' the Chief continued, still smiling because he'd had his moment of triumph, 'if Wainright *is* telling the truth and the man does hold a car-park pass, then we'll find him, won't we? Unfortunately we'll have to wait until tomorrow to find out.'

Markham spent most of Sunday in a foul mood, which was exacerbated by a raging hangover and the accompanying feelings of self-disgust. He was fed up with his dump of a flat, fed up with the job and depressed because of his almost non-existent social life. He was a few pints a day man but last night, after returning from the Prince William, it had seemed like a good idea to finish the last four inches of a bottle of Jack Daniels. He was hoping the alcohol would help him see things more clearly but all the exercise had achieved was a headache and a dry mouth. He sat drinking black coffee, not so much for medicinal purposes but because the milk was off. He, too, was reduced to making lists, albeit mental ones. The flats/video. The warehouse/ videos. Charlie/wasteground/near JC Warehousing. Charlie/St Hilda's Walk. What was the connection? He was certain there was one.

Madelaine Chambers was not expecting her husband back so early but Christopher had been in an odd, uncommunicative mood for the past forty-eight hours. There was definitely something on his mind.

Once she would have accompanied him to the golf club, but she no longer did so. The atmosphere between them was strained. She was aware of her own shortcomings when it came to relationships. Overt displays of affection dismayed her and her inability to express her feelings made her seem cold and unresponsive. She left that sort of thing to Christopher and the habit was now too strong to allow her to ask him what was wrong.

When he returned, damp-haired and grim-faced, she was speaking to her brother, long distance, on the telephone. She raised her eyebrows questioningly. Christopher shook his head and went upstairs.

'Sorry,' she said into the receiver. 'I missed that. Look, do you mind if I ring you back later?'

She said goodbye, hesitated at the foot of the stairs then went up. 'I'm just getting lunch,' she said through the closed door of his bedroom. 'It won't take long.' There was an unintelligible mutter which Madelaine did not query. If he had something to tell her, he would do so in his own time. She knew that if the roles were reversed she would have resented the interruption of self-imposed solitude.

She placed a lid on a saucepan without a single twinge of anxiety which might have prompted her to try again with her husband. Alone, upstairs, he came to his final decision. One which he believed would cause the least distress to his wife, whom, despite what he'd done, he loved more than anything in the world, and far, far more than she ever knew.

9

Charlie's killer spent a relaxed weekend, quietly laughing up his sleeve at the police. He was sure they would catch him in the end but they seemed to be taking a long time about it. Meanwhile he was thinking of a way to help them with another crime. Not for his sake. No, it was too late for him, but for the sake of others. It might be one way to redeem a little of the harm he had done over the years.

'I think,' the Chief said, 'we'll also treat this as an exercise in public relations.'

The air in the general office was already blue with cigarette smoke and the noisome odour of a cheap cigar brought back from a Spanish holiday. It became bluer with the expletives of the men dealing with serious crimes and not in the mood to wipe the bottoms of the public.

'Haven't we got enough on our plates, sir?' DC Emmanuel asked as politely as he was able.

'Maybe, but if you can impress people even when you're under pressure think how easy it'll be when you're not.'

'Yeah, well. At least with my looks and charm the public'll fall over themselves to be of assistance.'

'The female ones,' someone at the back said.

'That's for different reasons.' Winston Emmanuel jutted his pelvis forward lewdly.

The laughter that followed took the edge off the tension in the room. The Chief joined in. This was serious stuff – most of what they did was serious, some of it dangerous and parts of it sickening. Without moments of light relief they would not be able to cope.

'Okay, settle down. You may not all have Mr Emmanuel's allure, but a bit of diplomacy still won't go amiss. I know it's boring and I realise no one's going to be happy to be seen a second time, but it has to be done.' He detailed some men to go back to St Hilda's Walk with copies of an identikit of the man Wainright claimed to have seen talking to Charlie. He must be found, even if only to be eliminated. Markham was instructed to continue his attempts to find the connection he was so sure of whilst pressing on with his investigation into the robbery. 'I'm going back to the hospital. The Philpotts girl is awake now. You take over, Barry. Markham's theory has got me going. I want to check out a couple of things before I leave.'

During the night a thought had come to him, if it was a thought. It may have been part of a dream, something in the lower layers of his subconscious trying to reach the surface. He was no clearer than Markham, but he, too, was strongly beginning to believe there was a connection. The idea, the thing niggling him, just would not surface. Instead, not quite knowing why, he asked for a list of all the firms occupying office space in St Hilda's Walk. Later, if necessary, he wanted to know the names of every employee. But not just yet. Mandy Philpotts first.

Markham took himself off on foot to the industrial estate. The buildings there were low and flat-roofed, two storeys high at most. They were surrounded by Lombardy poplars which served both as a windbreak and to disguise the ugliness of the place. For all its modern architecture and the twee, double lampstands with their coloured glass globes, it still looked exactly what it was. It was pretentiously called The Poplars Business Park.

The rain was light but deceptive, penetrating Markham's clothes faster than he anticipated. His short, springy hair held a web of minute beads of water. He waited to cross the dual carriageway, not bothering to walk as far as the pedestrian lights. Tyres hissed as cars sped past, their headlights brightening the gloom. He saw his chance and dived across to the central reservation. He straddled it then waited again. He made it to the far side in the next break of traffic.

'Silly thing to do, young man,' an elderly lady in a very wet mac and a tea-cosy hat told him.

'Yeah, well,' he replied with a shrug and a lop-sided smile. She shook her head and went on her way, unaware that she had been the recipient of what passed for tact and good manners on Markham's part.

JC Warehousing was tucked away at the back, which had made it easier for the thieves. Large doors, several feet off the ground, were open, a container lorry backed up to the ramp. Two men in overalls were supervising the unloading and checking off of goods. Markham watched with interest. From where he stood he saw at least six men involved in the operation. How many others, then, knew where the videos and camcorders were? The staff here, the manufacturers, the transport company, and the security firm which was responsible for the alarm system and the guard.

He went round to a projecting reception area, mostly glass, with a notice asking visitors to report to the desk. He did so, showing his identity to the girl behind it. She hardly glanced at it, recalling him from a previous visit.

Instead she looked at him appreciatively, tossing her long hair over one shoulder, before picking up the internal phone. Markham ignored the look, then had second thoughts. She was very pretty. It was time he took a woman out again – he might ask her on his way out.

David Payne came out to greet him. 'Two coffees, please, Michelle,' he said as he showed Markham into his office. 'Made any progress?' Payne was not really optimistic.

'Not unless you count one machine.'

'You've found one? Where?'

'Here. In Rickenham. Don't build your hopes up, Mr Payne. I'm pretty certain the rest are out of the area.'

Payne glanced up as Michelle came in bearing a tray with two mugs of coffee and a sugar bowl. She placed it on the desk. Markham winked at her. She gave another toss of the silky hair and wiggled back out to her desk. Markham dug a spoon into the sugar, which consisted of hardened, tea-stained chunks.

'I know it's a bore, but could we just go through it all one more time?' The Chief, had he been able to hear, would have had to give him credit for diplomacy.

David Payne repeated his side of the story. All the facts remained unchanged. The night-watchman had been cleared. Initially he was the main cause for concern.

'No need to inform the insurance company, I suppose?' Payne asked when the interview was over. They had taken long enough to pay out as it was; he didn't want to give them any more grounds for delay.

'No. In fact, I'd prefer it if you didn't mention this to anyone at the moment.'

'Suits me.'

Another possibility that had been followed up was insurance fraud, but it wasn't really likely: only the manufacturers stood to gain. And not even that. They would receive compensation but lose business because of it. But there was one angle they had not looked at, or at least, not in the right way. Markham read his notes, checked one important fact again, then left. His head was reeling with the possibility of what he might have come up with. He didn't even acknowledge Michelle's farewell as he left the building.

'What the hell have we got here?' the Chief said after he had given Barry time to read and digest the report from Forensics. Stomach analysis and blood, etc. were just as would be expected, but the fingernail scrapings told a different story. There were minute traces of heroin. They were also to be found in his pocket. Ian clutched his head as if it would help his thinking.

'We have our man living in squalor and according to his mates he mostly doesn't have the money for a drink, yet he's in possession of drugs. Hang on. Golding's statement. Didn't he mention drugs? Get it for me, will you?'

But there was no mention of drugs. 'No,' Ian remembered, 'it was as he was on his way out.' He had made a note of it himself later. For what purpose he was not sure at the time, but it certainly wasn't because he thought Charlie was involved with them. 'I can't afford drugs now,' Golding had said, 'even if I knew where to get them.' Did it really mean anything, though, or was there more to those words than could be guessed at?

'There are far too many coincidences here. We have a badly beaten girl who's a user, we have Charlie dead – okay, no proof that he ever touched the stuff himself, but he had it on him – and we have a man in a suit who, if Wainwright is to be believed, handed him something.'

'Which might possibly be crack.'

'Exactly.'

106

'Don't forget Wainright. He travels abroad.'

'Mm. Anything on Danny Grant yet?'

'No, the Met haven't come back to us. I've contacted Felixstowe as well. There might be something on him there. What next?'

'You tell me.'

Markham flung himself through the swing doors, breathless and wet, only to learn he had missed the Chief by seconds. 'Perhaps', DS William Baker said laconically from behind his desk when Markham finished cursing, 'you might make more use of that modern invention, the motor car.'

'Sod off, Baker. Is Swan around?'

'Yep.'

'Right.'

Markham wanted to go it alone, to follow his instincts, but he accepted that that was not the way things were done. If they all followed their own noses without discussing things as a team it was unlikely any progress would be made.

He decided to find out a little more about Allways Security in Ipswich.

'Nil,' Barry told Ian when he returned from Rickenham General. 'Same story as Philpotts. Grant's parents still live at the address in Lewisham. He left with Mandy and hasn't been heard of since, and, according to London, his parents would prefer it to stay that way. But no previous, not known on the drugs scene.'

'Philpotts won't talk and her parents can't come up with anything else. She's had no other visitors, not even the girls she shares with. And I find that odd. Right. Anything moving elsewhere?'

'No. No one seems to know anything about our mystery man in St Hilda's Walk, but you know what these identikits are like, and Wainright couldn't be expected to get more than an impression.'

'I think we'll pay him a visit. Later, in his own home, and I don't think we'll bother to warn him in advance. Now, reverting to Markham's theory. Is there a connection between Charlie, Philpotts and our suited man, and is all, or any, of this relevant to the missing videos? I've asked for a list of all the companies occupying the office blocks and their exact business. I have a strong suspicion Markham is right.'

By the end of the day he was certain he was.

'Sir . . . Oh sorry.'

The Chief was on the telephone. He indicated a chair and Markham sat down.

'You were right,' he said when he replaced the receiver, 'or at least it looks that way.' The Chief then told him what he had discovered. Markham's face said it all. He knew why the man in front of him was a Chief Inspector and he was a DS. He had wasted his time driving to Ipswich and talking to the Allways Security people. Yes, he got the information he was after, but the Chief had done it from this end with a telephone call from the comfort of his own office.

'Better find someone and go and pick him up.'

'Yes, sir.' At least the arrest would be down to him.

'So,' Barry recapped as they drove towards Wainright's house, 'Chambers worked for Allways, then, out of the blue, takes a job with a different security firm in Rickenham. And Allways are responsible for security at JC Warehousing.'

'But the break-in didn't occur until after Chambers left, so it's possible he set it up, then got out before it could be traced to him.'

'Possible, not certain. But Chambers' reasons for leaving didn't ring true. Who gives up a secure job in this day and age to go to work for a newly founded company which might not succeed?'

'I like it.'

'What?'

'Secure job?'

'Pun unintended. Are you listening to me or not?'

'Don't I always? Get it, Allways?'

'What's the matter with you tonight? And don't tell me if it involves anything you and young Lucy get up to.'

'All right. But why are we calling on Wainright?'

'For a start, we might need him for a positive ID. Secondly, I'm curious.' He refused to say anything further.

Wainright's semi-detached house was situated in one of the better districts of the town and was well looked after. The short gravel drive was weed-free, the borders edging the grass were bare now and the soil had already been turned over in heavy clumps ready for the frost to break up. The paintwork was fresh and unchipped and the red tiles in the outer porch looked as if they were regularly scrubbed. But spoiling the effect of what should have been a desirable Victorian villa were mullioned bay windows which had not been included in the architect's original plans. Behind these, incongruously, hung flounced, pink nets.

None of this was in keeping with what Barry knew of Wainright. He was prissy and obviously took great pains with his clothes but there was a plainness about them, nothing flashy, nothing ostentatious. The nets must be the handiwork of his wife, and Barry was interested to meet her. Underneath Wainright's outward manner he suspected there lay something sleazy.

The door was opened by a woman who informed them she was Mrs Wainright and asked what they wanted with her husband. She was painfully thin, her face untouched by make-up. Her only jewellery was a wedding ring which slipped loosely round her finger as she reached out a hand to inspect their identification.

Barry Swan, who considered himself an expert in the field, thought a plainer woman could not exist. Everything about her was grey – her hair, her clothes, her skin – and if she had ever smiled there was no evidence of it now.

'I'm right in the middle of preparing our evening meal. Come back later if you wish to see Basil.'

'I'm afraid we can't do that, Mrs Wainright. We are conducting a murder inquiry. We need to see him now. Of course, if it's inconvenient for you, having us here, he can come down to the station to answer our questions.' There was a pause while she considered the implication of those words.

'I suppose you'd better come in. It looks dreadful having people hanging around on the doorstep. Is that your car?' She nodded towards the Rover. It was unmarked.

'It is. Is it likely to cause an obstruction there?'

'No.' Ian and Barry each telepathically knew what the other was thinking: Mrs Wainright had checked because she didn't want the neighbours to know the police had come a-calling.

'What do you want with Basil?' she asked as she showed them into the living-room.

Neither man answered. Temporarily they were unable to. 'Would you fetch him for us, please.' They knew he was at home; his car was in the drive.

They had cringed in unison when they entered the room. As if to make up for her own lack of femininity every movable object had been prettified. The effect was suffocating. Flowers were the predominant theme. Chair backs, runners, little mats under vases holding the artificial variety, all were embroidered with roses and tulips and coloured daisies. Others were crocheted in pink or lilac silk. Porcelain shepherdesses, of the vacuously smiling species, littered every surface. Ian bet himself a pound that the spare toilet roll was camouflaged with a knitted poodle but did not think he'd be allowed the opportunity to find out if he had to pay himself.

Mrs Wainright stood amongst the dainty, girlish objects. It did not seem possible she was responsible for them. Her arms were folded tightly across her chest, her lips were clamped tightly together. 'He's just coming down. He was having a wash before his meal.'

Point taken, the Chief thought. This was not a house where meals were late. Barry felt sorry for Wainright, remembering the interview and how he said his wife hadn't spoken to him. On the other hand, he hadn't been exactly truthful either.

The door opened and Wainright appeared. He may well have just washed but there were beads of sweat along his upper lip and they were not caused by the heat from the two-bar electric fire in its mock marble surround.

'Good evening. Detective Sergeant Swan, isn't it?'

'Hello, Mr Wainright. This is Chief Inspector Roper.'

Wainwright swallowed noisily at the introduction of the senior policeman.

'We'd like a few words, if you don't mind,' the Chief said, casting a glance in the direction of his wife. If he didn't want her to hear, now was his chance to say so.

'Oh, er, have a seat, gentlemen.'

Mrs Wainright sniffed her disapproval. There was no need for them to get comfortable.

'I wonder if you'd mind going over what you told us yesterday, down at the station.' The Chief was spelling it out, watching Mrs Wainright's face for her reaction. She remained stoically rooted to the spot, no change of expression. She was aware of his visit, then.

'I can't think anything I told you was unclear. However, I'll do so if you wish.' He relaxed slightly.

He repeated, almost verbatim, what he had told Barry, who was now out of his line of vision. Covering the same ground twice, telling it to a different person, sometimes gave rise to a different version. Not so much in factual content but in the slant of the emphasis. This was not the case here.

Wainright said he worked for a market research company which occupied one floor of the office block. The company moved there because of expansion and had taken on new staff. Wainright was not one of them. He had had the same job for nine years.

'Just out of curiosity, Mr Wainright, I know nothing about market research, but tell me, how come your job takes you overseas?'

There was a faint pinkness creeeping up the lobes of Wainright's ears. The Chief wondered whether it was caused by guilt or embarrassment. Sizing up the man, and his wife, he had a fair idea of what he might get up to on his trips. It was not a bad thing to let a suspect think you were ignorant. Few could resist putting a police officer straight, and in doing so they might give a bit too much away.

'Well, we, that is, my company, act on an international basis. Foreign manufacturers and suppliers need to be aware of what's going on over here. You see, certain products sell far better in some areas than others. We tell

112

them where to place the goods. Most of this is done by phone or fax but now and then either myself or one of my colleagues goes over. It always pays to keep your face in the picture. And it helps to know who you're dealing with personally. To be perfectly honest, the travel is one of the perks of the job. There aren't many around these days.'

'Ah. I see. Thank you. And you arrived back on Thursday?'

The pinkness was darker and Wainright could do nothing about it. 'No, Friday night, wasn't it, dear?' Interesting that he needed his wife to confirm it. More interesting, he was lying.

'Thank you for your time, Mr Wainright.'

The Chief stood up. Wainright's expression changed to one of relief as he and Barry showed signs of leaving. He darted across the room to show them out. Mrs Wainright disappeared to the nether regions of the house where, presumably, the kitchen was.

On the doorstep the Chief hesitated. 'Strange,' he commented with a bland smile. 'I might be mistaken, but I'm sure your company told me you returned to work on Friday.'

He stepped on to the drive but his feet making contact with the gravel did not drown Wainright's desperate groan.

'I'm sorry? Did you say something?'

Wainright came on to the steps and pulled the door almost closed behind him. He was oblivious of the rain soaking his shirt. 'I was there. At work. I didn't think you'd check. I mean, I haven't done anything, not anything to do with that man's murder.'

'You'd better get your jacket. I think your dinner's going to have to wait.'

*

'What's keeping Markham? He's had more than enough time to pick Chambers up.'

'He might be away on business,' Barry suggested.

'Message for you, sir.' A PC handed him a note.

'That's all we need. He's done a bunk. Didn't turn up at work today and, according to Markham, his wife knows nothing about it. She says he went off as usual this morning.'

'Why wait until now?'

'He must know we've been asking questions. Come on, let's have a chat with Wainright. He's sweated enough by now.'

Wainright, once he started talking, could not stop and left Ian feeling more like a priest than a policeman.

'My wife, well, you've met her, she only puts up with sex because she feels it's her duty in return for my supplying her with a house and money. Once a month, Chief Inspector. Every four weeks on a Friday and she changes the sheets the next day. It's humiliating really, but I'd never divorce her. Neither of us has anyone else. Our parents are dead, she's an only child and my sister's in Canada. We didn't have any children because she was too terrified of the experience. I know I'm not much to look at so I go with prostitutes.' He was almost crying when he made the admission. 'An affair wasn't on, even supposing I could find anyone. You probably won't understand when I say that would somehow seem more disloyal. This way I'm simply paying for something I can't get at home. It's easier when I'm abroad, in fact they're sometimes provided as part of the entertainment.'

'And here, at home?'

'I use one of the local girls. Oh God, it's awful. We don't go back to her place and I wouldn't dare risk it in the car. My wife, you see, would be bound to spot even one stray hair.'

'So what do you do, Mr Wainright? Take them down some back alley?'

Wainright nodded. 'Whatever must you think of me?'

'We are not interested in your sexual behaviour, it's a man's death which concerns us. How did you come across these girls?'

'It was accidental really. A few years ago I came into some money and I invested it in property hoping to make a killing. The plan backfired. At the moment the place wouldn't reach anything like I paid for it. I rent it out. No, that's not strictly true. That was my intention. The young man who wanted it said he knew of a couple of girls who wanted to share. He must have known, he must have seen the sort of person I am. He suggested that in return for the accommodation, instead of him paying rent, I could use the services of the girls whenever I wanted. It was perfect. My wife wouldn't be able to spot I'd been spending more cash than usual and I didn't stand to lose anything really. The house is in my name and paid for, it's still an asset. They have to pay all the bills there.'

'If your wife is so fully cognisant of your financial affairs, surely she would expect to see some rent money?'

'No. She thinks its empty. She doesn't drive, you see, and there's nothing in that part of Rickenham, I mean, no shops or anything. She has no reason to go near the place.'

'If she finds out?'

'I don't know. I really don't know.'

'Okay, Mr Wainright. Where exactly is this house?'

'Do I have to tell you?'

'I think you do.'

The address Wainright gave made Ian and Barry draw in their breath.

'Do you know anyone by the name of Amanda Philpotts? Mandy Philpotts?'

Wainright's face was now ashen. He was in deeper than he thought.

'One of the girls is called Mandy. I don't know her other name.'

'And did you know that she is in hospital after receiving a severe beating?'

'No.' Ian saw he was telling the truth.

'Did you know she uses hard drugs?'

'Oh, Jesus, no.'

'I'm afraid so. We'd like to know where she gets them. You have plenty of opportunity, travelling around as you do. Do you supply her, Mr Wainright?'

'No. What do you take me for?'

Ian declined to answer.

'I think he's telling the truth, about not knowing Philpotts is in hospital and the drugs. What do you think?' Ian said later.

'I agree. But here we go again. Wainright now fits into the picture. Surely they can't all be in something together.'

'Let me think. Wainright went to Brussels on Tuesday but he was here when Charlie was killed. It was also on that Tuesday that Philpotts admitted herself to hospital. Is he lying? Had he perhaps told her he was going but no more supplies would be forthcoming? And then we have the fact that Wainright told his wife he was away until Friday when he was actually back on Thursday. And it's Friday night that Philpotts gets beaten up.'

'Yes, but that was in the small hours. Mrs Wainright confirmed he was home by about ten and I'm pretty certain that lady is straight to the point. If he said ten and it was later, she'd've wanted to know about it.'

'Let's leave it for now, it's all too much to take in. Has Chambers turned up yet?'

'How should I know? I've been interviewing with you for the last half-hour or more.'

'I think what we'll do is get Markham back here, let Mrs Chambers think the coast is clear, but I'll get a couple of men on surveillance.'

Ian did just that then made a second call, this one to Moira. 'I'll be about an hour,' he said, 'and I think I'm going to need a stiff drink.'

Moira said he'd have to pour it himself; she was going out for a Chinese with her friend, Deirdre.

Ian waited until Markham was back. 'He hasn't contacted his office at all. They were very surprised, they said Chambers was very reliable. The same applied at Allways in Ipswich. He never took time off sick, or for any other reason, so it's got to be serious. Mrs Chambers swears she knows nothing about any of it but she did say her husband had not been himself for a couple of days. I asked her his reasons for changing jobs. She didn't really seem to know.'

'Perhaps she didn't care.'

'She gives that impression. An ice maiden. But she was genuinely distressed at his disappearance. I'll go and see the bloke at Allways again tomorrow, find out exactly what Chambers' role was and how much he'd know about JC Warehousing.'

'Good. And Markham – well done.'

The corner of Markham's mouth twitched. Ian could only assume it was a smile.

'Turn that bloody thing down, will you?' These were the first words Ian addressed to his son when he arrived home on Monday night. He could not explain his change of mood; all he knew was that his earlier optimism had evaporated by the time he reached home. Had Moira been in the room she would have reminded him with a reproachful glance that Mark, too, had an existence of his own and that the world did not, as he occasionally let himself believe, revolve around Ian Roper, however hard a day it had been. But Moira was out enjoying herself with Deirdre.

Mark, who was as eloquent as his mother, without saying a word, unhooked one ankle from the opposite knee, stood up and switched off the television then left the room, shutting the door behind him very quietly, very deliberately.

'Oh, hell, what've I done now?' Ian asked himself as he sat down with his whisky glass and took off his shoes.

10

Surveillance was established outside the Chambers's house, unknown to Madelaine. Markham returned to the station. Although a man was posted at both the back and the front of the house, this would not prevent her contacting her husband by telephone. Markham was convinced, however, that she really was unaware of his whereabouts, that her distress was genuine.

'I've rung everyone we know,' she confessed, which in itself must have cost the cold, confident beauty quite a lot of pride. 'Things haven't been right between us for months. I suspected there might be somebody else.' It might be true, Christopher Chambers might have a mistress into whose arms he had fled, but why not go to work as usual unless he knew they were on to him?

Markham made notes and left a copy for the Chief for the morning, then took himself off to the Prince William.

In the far corner, muffled up in a coat and scarf, sat George Miller slowly sipping a half of mild. When he saw Markham he dropped the cigarette he was about to light. It rolled off the table and on to the floor. Markham went across and picked it up.

'Nervous?'

'Why should I be? I've told you everything I know.'

'Maybe. We'll see.' Markham returned to where his drink stood waiting on the bar. He, too, sipped it slowly, the memory of yesterday's hangover not quite forgotten. He glanced at the clock behind the bar. Time for a second pint and then home. Tonight he'd be lazy and get a take-away pizza with a selection from the salad bar. He was short on vegetables lately.

As he was finishing his drink another man entered the bar. He was of medium height, casually dressed, but in clothes that did not come cheaply. Even before he spoke he had a swaggering manner. Markham put him in his mid-thirties. Then he wondered why he had made these observations. Like all police officers he was trained to observe but some sixth sense told him this was a villain, and one he did not recognise. He looked over at Miller, who was studying the contents of his glass. Miller knew him. There was little he could do, this was 'his' pub, where he met his informant, where gossip was to be picked up concerning the local criminal fraternity. If he started asking questions his sources of information would dry up. He ordered another half and covertly studied the man. He was all joviality and back-thumping with the man he was standing next to, yet Markham got the impression the second man hardly knew him. After one quick short the man left.

'See you, Alex,' the landlord said as he departed.

Markham turned to him. 'I might as well have the other half,' he said, feeling in his pocket for a handful of change. When his glass was replenished he handed over the money, deliberately dropping some of the coins on to the counter. The landlord was a suspicious man, probably because he did a bit of short-changing him-self. He carefully checked the coins and Markham said casually, 'Remind me, Albert, what's old Alex's last name?'

'Chambers,' he said, without looking up. Then, realis-ing too late what he'd said, he slung the cash into the till in disgust. Markham grinned. He knew Albert's policy of playing dumb. If his customers wanted to grass one another up, fine, but Albert knew nothing.

Markham went home via the Pizza Hut. Another coincidence, he thought as he filled a plastic container with salad, is really not on.

DS Barry Swan had to cancel a date with Lucy, who took the news with far more equanimity than he liked but he supposed that, as she was a long-standing friend of Judy Robbins, she knew what the job entailed. Lucy herself worked in a bank and kept far more regular hours. However, it was Judy who was to accompany him to Saxborough Road where Mandy Philpotts and her flat-mates lived. He would have the consolation of talking about Lucy. But Judy was in one of her most infuriating moods.

'Why do you always drive like a prick?' she asked as he took a bend too fast.

Barry's face reddened. 'I don't always. It's probably the company I'm in.' They continued the journey in strained silence.

Saxborough Road was in the main thoroughfare out of the town on the northern side. It was two-laned, but wide, punctuated with sets of traffic lights and groupings of bollards. The large houses lining it had once been family homes but were now mostly converted into flats and bedsits. With a large, pale moon high in the sky and the glow of the street lights casting shadows off the bare branches of the trees, the area did not look as seedy as it actually was.

Barry turned into a side street where there was only a single yellow line and parked. He and Judy approached number 37. There was a flight of steps leading to the basement. Litter flapped around the dustbins. On the sturdy front door was a lion's head knocker, stiff with

121

rust and no longer in use for on the right was a row of buzzers, the names of the residents typed or written beside them. They rang Flat 5.

Sheila Dixon told them to come up. The stair carpet was threadbare but clean and held down by what might have been the original carpet rods. The door of Flat 5 was painted deep purple and a white plastic number was screwed into it. The door opened straight into the main living area and although Barry did not quite know what he had expected, it was not what he saw. The furnishings were heavy and solid and there was a piano in one corner of the large room. On it were framed photographs. It was the room of a genteel spinster getting on in years. No one would guess three modern young women lived here.

Barry introduced WPC Robbins and they were offered a seat and a cup of tea. They accepted the first and refused the second.

'This is Marie O'Doyle,' Sheila Dixon said.

'How is Mandy?' Marie's first words gained her some credit in Barry's eyes.

'Improving. Haven't you been to see her?'

'I . . . No, we haven't had time.' It was hard to believe but he made a mental note of the words, which were spoken in a gentle Irish lilt.

'We're here because one or two things aren't quite clear. If you don't mind, we'd like you to tell us again exactly what happened on Friday night. Actually,' he continued, 'I think I'd like that tea.'

Sheila looked at Marie. Some silent communication passed between them. It was Marie who went out to the kitchen. Barry had decided it might be better to get one version at a time but he was also sure it was Sheila who remained to answer the questions because she was the stronger of the two. In which case, they had something to hide.

'All right, Sheila, tell me what happened.'

'We'd all been out on Friday night, but not together. Marie was with her boyfriend, I was with my own friends. I don't know where Mandy went but she got ready to go out about eight.'

'And did she go out then?'

'No. Not until about quarter past nine. She watched something on television first.'

'So she left after you and Marie?'

'No. We all caught the same bus into town. A number twelve,' she added, watching Judy jot it down in her notebook. Sheila Dixon was no fool. She would supply them with detailed information which might have no relevance to the case and which might also throw them off the track.

'And when you got into town, what did you do then?'

'Marie was meeting her boyfriend in the Three Feathers then they were going on to the Nite Spot. I was meeting my friends in the Three Bells so I took the opposite direction. Look, do you relly need to know all this?'

Judy Robbins caught Barry's eye. She was thinking the same thing. Why stop there?

'It might help jog your memory if you go over the whole evening. Ah, tea. Thanks.'

There was a hiatus whilst the cups were distributed and sugar offered. Barry put his cup on the small table beside him and picked up a photograph. It was of Sheila in a 1920s costume.

'She was an actress,' Marie said, almost proudly. 'Look, this one's when she had a part in *The Sound of Music*.'

Sheila almost snatched it from her. 'That was ages ago, I was just a kid.' She replaced it on the piano.

Barry got back to the matter in hand. 'When did each of you return home?' They had already checked with neighbours. None had either seen the girls' return or heard any of the later events.

'You've asked us that before. Like I said, about midnight. If you must know, I made a cup of coffee and went straight to bed. It had been a long week.'

'Hectic at work?'

She looked at him steadily and seemed to come to some sort of decision. 'All right, if you must know, we all do casual work. No tax, no stamps. Are you going to arrest us?'

'Why should I?'

'It's illegal, isn't it?'

'Not necessarily, not if your earnings are low enough.' The girls' earnings were not the question in point. Another red herring had been thrown his way.

'How much is the rent here?'

'Not very much at all. A friend lets us use it as a favour.'

'I see.' He was not going to pursue this line of questioning. If he did so now and caught her out in a lie, she would clam up. Mandy's attacker was what he was after. Neither did he ask exactly how and where they all managed to get enough casual labour to live on. He also knew the answer to that. For the time being he needed Marie and Sheila to think they had nothing to fear.

'Marie? Can you tell us about your Friday night?'

'To be sure I can. I had a bath, just before Mandy wanted to use the bathroom, then I caught the bus with Sheila and Mandy and we all went into Rickenham. I met Dave, that's my boyfriend, at the Three Feathers. We had two drinks there, it wasn't very busy, then we went to the Nite Spot. It was packed there, well now, it normally is on Fridays, and it was very noisy. I had a headache so I came home earlier than usual and went to bed.'

'Dave bring you back?'

124

'No. He stayed on once he'd got a taxi for me.'

'What time would that've been?'

'I'm not sure. But it was before twelve.' As she spoke her voice rose, as if she was seeking confirmation from Sheila that this was so.

'And Sheila was already home?'

'Yes.' It was said with finality.

'Let's get back to Mandy now. What can you tell us about her?'

'What sort of thing?' Marie asked.

'Anything that comes to mind. Her friends, her personality, her past.'

'As far as I know,' Sheila interrupted, 'we were her only friends. She hasn't been here long. I met her through a mutual acquaintance. She was looking for somewhere to stay and a job. We have a spare room here so it seemed logical she shared with us. She said her boyfriend had ditched her, that he'd got work on a boat in Felixstowe. At first she believed it was because he wanted enough money so's they could get married. Then she realised what he'd really done.' Sheila was talking more easily now. Barry recognised the truth in what she was saying. 'She's had a bad time. Her parents threw her out because of this boy, then he dumps her. And now look what's happened.'

So that was the story Mandy was putting about. What she said about her parents was a lie; perhaps the boyfriend story was too.

'What's she like, to live with?'

Marie shook her head. 'She's hard to get to know. She's tidy and does her share, but she's not a great one for a chat. What do you think, Sheila?'

'She's a close one all right. Not like when she first came here. But she's pleasant enough.'

Judy watched Sheila. She was blonde and pretty and well proportioned but there were already furrows of discontent in her young face and a sourness about the mouth. In ten years' time she would look another decade older than her actual age. Marie was a different matter. A cloud of dark hair framed her face. Her nose was freckled and her mouth suggested a predisposition to laughter. Her speech and manner were gentle and Judy thought she belonged back amongst the green fields and the mountains of her native Ireland. It was a waste.

'One last thing,' Barry said as he stood up to leave. 'Where did Mandy get the heroin?'

'We didn't know. Honestly. Not until your people came here searching.'

'I never even guessed,' Marie added. 'I suppose we weren't looking for signs. I still find it hard to believe.'

'She never mentioned it? Never tried to get either of you on it?'

They both denied it. Again Barry thought they were speaking the truth. 'Thank you. That's it for now. We'll let you know if we need to talk to you again.'

Sheila showed them out and they descended the stairs.

'Do you believe it? That they didn't know about her habit?' Judy asked, their earlier disagreement forgotten.

'It seems unlikely, but, yes, I do. What was more revealing was that Mandy comes across as a selfish little madam.'

'I agree. Where do you think they pick up their men?'

'You tell me. In bars, clubs, off the street. No, we'd know them. Perhaps they have regular clients.'

'Like Wainright.'

'Like Wainright.'

By that time they were back at the station.

During the night, having blown away the rain clouds, the wind dropped. The first, early ground frost fell. It was not heavy enough to blacken the late autumn flowers but was a warning of things to come.

The morning dawned dry and chilly but the sky was blue and a pale lemon sun shone at a low angle. Ian drove to work wondering whether Mark's silence this morning over breakfast was due to his own abrupt words of last night or his son's natural morning truculence.

'Report on the interviews with Philpotts' flatmates,' Barry said, the minute Ian walked in. He handed him a sheaf of papers. 'And Markham's report on Christopher Chambers and his wife. Oh, by the way, Philpotts is wide awake and demanding food.'

'Yes, very good, Swan, but let's get our priorities right. Coffee first. Anyway, what's got you in here so early?'

'A good night's sleep.' He winked, leaving Ian in no doubt as to what he meant.

Barry returned with two mugs of coffee. 'Leaving Wainright out of this for the moment, this thing with Chambers – what made you think it was him?'

'Not him. Anyone in the offices. Markham also thought there was a connection to do with St Hilda's Walk. He investigated it from a different angle. He knew Allways Security covered JC Warehousing and believed it might be someone within that company who was passing on information. Who would be in a better position to know the easiest way to get into the place? He discovered Chambers had left and come to work in Rickenham Green, and at another security firm who just happen to have premises in St Hilda's Walk.'

'Fine. I can go along with that. But how did you see it?'

'I was looking at it from the angle of Charlie's death. Working on the assumption that he was blackmailing someone, and that St Hilda's Walk was his patch, it was more than likely to be someone who worked there. Now, most of the firms who moved in did so because they're expanding.'

'Well, go on.'

Ian was fumbling in his desk drawer hoping to find a packet of cigarettes. 'Give me one of your fags, will you?' Once it was lit he continued, 'I asked myself where all the extra staff came from.'

'Obvious, I'd've thought. Unemployed, people moving from other places for more money or promotion.'

'Yes, but rule them out and what are you left with?'

'Well, tell me.'

'Someone who changed jobs because they had to, because they were in danger of being found out. It wasn't hard to check. Most of the firms brought along most of their old staff, it was only the additional ones we needed to look at. I soon discovered that Chambers left a longstanding career, one with a pension etc., for one wih a lower salary. Only very slightly lower, I accept, but why do it at all if there was no advantage to be had? Once I knew where he'd worked before, I put two and two together. Not that it gets us any farther forward. We still have to prove Chambers was involved.'

'And you believe he killed Charlie because Charlie knew what he'd been up to? How could he know? Allways is in Ipswich.'

'That's what's baffling me. But then, I'm not saying it was Chambers who killed him, or, at least, made one of the attempts.'

'And according to Markham, Chambers' wife simply believes he's run off with another woman.'

'He may have done that as well. Bugger off now, I want to read these reports.'

11

It did not take Markham long to gather sufficient evidence
to enable them to arrest Christopher Chambers when he
was found. Allways Security supplied a short list of premises covered by themselves which had been broken into
during the course of the past twelve months. Chambers
was responsible for advising on security for all but two.
The properties were scattered within a wide radius and
were of varying types, but there had not been enough of
them for it to appear suspicious to the board of directors.
Their annual average of such events had not increased
drastically and they had put it down to the rise in crime.

Chambers had now had a day's grace and could be
almost anywhere. One consolation was that his wife
confirmed his passport was still in his desk, although
this did not rule out his obtaining a fake one.

Chambers' role at Allways had been to advise on and
arrange for the installation of the appropriate security
devices required by their clients, often on the advice of
their insurance companies. No one, therefore, had more
intimate knowledge of how to overcome these devices.

Markham was about to type up his latest findings
when the Chief told him to go and see Madelaine
Chambers and find out what the name Alex Chambers
meant to her. Like Markham, the Chief thought this was
one coincidence too many.

*

For once there were plenty of spaces in the hospital car-park. 'Good morning, Sister,' Ian said when he trod the familiar path to intensive care. 'I believe Miss Philpotts is well enough to answer some questions now. Is it all right if I see her?'

'She's not here.'

Ian froze. Mandy had spent most of yesterday asleep, aided by large doses of painkillers, and she was badly injured. A WPC had not left her side; her parents were also with her. It was impossible they'd lost her again.

'Oh, don't worry,' the sister told him. 'I meant she's no longer under my care. She was moved to Jenner Ward this morning. Second floor, third on the right.' She smiled. 'We're not that careless twice, you know.' News of Mandy's initial disappearance had obviously passed efficiently through the hospital grapevine.

When he found Mandy's bed her parents were seated on either side of it. A WPC was also seated, trying to pretend she wasn't listening to the loving and encouraging words they spoke.

Mandy's eyes were closed but she was not asleep. Maybe it was the bruising and puffiness that made it painful for her to keep them open or else she was shutting out a world she wanted to know nothing about. Her mouth was red and swollen and, when she licked her dry lips, the Chief saw the two front teeth were broken. She altered her position slightly and groaned with the effort.

He asked Mr and Mrs Philpotts if they would mind waiting outside while he talked to their daughter.

'Of course not,' Mrs Philpotts replied. 'Anything, if it'll help find who did this.'

They left the ward, tiredness visible in their slow progress. The Chief mouthed a question at the WPC, who shook her head. Mandy was saying nothing.

'Mandy,' he said, taking the chair vacated by her

mother, 'my name is Ian Roper. I'm Detective Chief Inspector here in Rickenham. I realise how you must be feeling but I do have to ask you a few questions.' She made no response. 'If it hurts to speak, raise your arm if the answer's yes. Do you know who did this to you?'

He waited. There was no movement.

'I don't wish to seem unkind, but I find it hard to believe you and your friends were asleep and someone managed to get into both the house and your particular flat without leaving any signs of breaking and entering. Who let him in, Mandy? Was it you?'

He stopped. She was muttering something. He asked her to repeat it. He and the WPC leaned forward to catch the words. She was breathing rapidly. It was difficult to judge whether she was attractive because her face was so discoloured by her injuries. Her hair lay in lank clumps on the pillow.

'What did they say?'

'Who, Mandy? What did who say?'

'Marie. Sheila.'

The Chief would not lie to her. He simply said, 'They have both made statements.'

Mandy ignored any implication in his answer. 'Where's Danny?' she said. The 's' was sibilant, pronounced through the broken teeth.

'Danny? Your boyfriend?' Danny was supposed to be long off the scene.

She nodded, screwing up her face in pain.

'We don't know. We thought perhaps you could tell us. Is Danny the one who did this to you?'

'No.' Two tears slid from beneath the closed lids. 'Danny wouldn't.'

'All right, Mandy. But think about it. You know who did this to you and for what reason. He might not let it go at this. Next time could be worse.'

The tears continued to roll down her face. She did not

need to be told that. She had thought of nothing else, but was too terrified of what might become of her before her attacker was caught.

'I think that's enough for now. Excuse me, I'm John Peterson, Mandy's doctor. Mandy, I'm going to get the nurse to give you another painkiller.'

As they strolled down the ward the Chief asked when they might talk to her again. The doctor looked at his watch. 'She'll probably drop off for a couple of hours. Come back this evening. You'll see even more of an improvement. The young are amazingly resilient.'

The Chief thanked him and negotiated the maze of corridors and stairs until he was once more in the car-park. It was very cold after the unnatural warmth of the building.

'She's terrified of someone,' he said to Barry.

'I think the other two are as well. But we can't force them to talk.'

'Perhaps a female would get a better result. I'll send one along later.' It rankled with him that, in his view, there were still not enough women in CID, and, in his area, certainly not enough senior ones.

Barry was not in the best of moods either. Having broken their date last night he had fully expected to hear from Lucy today. So far she had not rung.

Ian had been back for almost an hour before Markham put in an appearance. 'Madelaine Chambers, sir, she says her husband has a cousin by that name, and although she doesn't have a photo, the description fits the man I saw. But she also told me they didn't get on well – like chalk and cheese, she said – but she still includes him on their Christmas card list. That's about the extent of the relationship.'

'Does she know where he lives?'

'London, she said.'

'London? Then what's he doing here? Find out, Markham, will you?'

'Sure. Here's his London address anyway.'

The Chief had only decided to allow Markham to follow up on Alex Chambers because, although the name was common enough, he trusted Markham's instinct. If he thought the man was a villain, he probably was.

'And this is where she sent the Christmas cards?'

'Yes, but it's getting on for a year now. He could have moved anywhere. He never sent one back.'

'But why come here? I'd like to know the answer to that. Get on to the DVLA, see if he's got a car licensed in his name. We might pick him up that way. Get on with it, then.'

'Yes, sir. Oh, I got this,' he added as he made for the door. He handed the Chief a six-by-four snapshot of a tall, well-dressed man in his late forties. The dark hair was greying at the edges, his features were clean cut. The setting was a garden ablaze with summer flowers. The subject was posed on a lichen-covered stone balustrade surrounding an impressive house. He was smiling straight at the camera, a contented and happy man.

'Christopher Chambers, taken two years ago outside their home. His wife says he's hardly altered.'

'Good. Let's hope Wainright can identify him as the man he saw talking to Charlie. Send Campbell up when you go.'

DC Alan Campbell arrived almost at once.

'A man named Grant, Danny Grant. I want him found. Last seen in London. Ran off with the Philpotts girl. There was a possible sighting in Felixstowe. Get on to Mandy's parents if you have to, they may know his old London address. He's early twenties, that's all we know. See what you can do.'

The female detective constable who was sent to see

133

Mandy Philpotts later that day had no more luck than the Chief. Their hands were tied. There was nothing which said she must name her attacker.

Danny Grant was safely out of it, doing what he was paid to do, knowing the risks involved. Lately he had begun to wonder how long it would be before he was caught. He wanted out but knew it was not possible. Had he known what had happened to Mandy he would have given himself up.

The fishing boat upon which he was employed was miles out at sea, quite legally making a catch, a better one than was expected. However, before it returned to land that catch, the crew had other business to attend to.

When Ian left the station at six forty-five there was still no news of either of the Chambers. Madelaine had rung several times, her anxiety apparent. She promised to get in touch immediately if she heard from her husband.

'Oh, good, you remembered,' Moira said when he came into the kitchen immediately he entered the house. He was in search of a beer. Moira usually managed to get in a couple of the plastic bottles of Adnams stocked by the supermarkets. It was not the same as a decent drop in the pub but he guessed her motives for doing it.

'Remembered what?' Not her birthday, that was circled clearly in red ink on the calendar on his desk at work. Was he supposed to pick something up for her?

'Oh, honestly, Ian. I told you this morning. Doc Harris and Shirley are coming over.'

This morning was a lifetime ago. 'Hold on, I thought I . . .' No, it was several days ago when he'd put the Doc off. The wives must have arranged this between themselves.

'What time are they coming?'

'About eight. You've got time for a shower. I've done a risotto, I've only got to heat it up.'

Although he could have done with a quiet evening, the Harrises' company was always enjoyable and at least Moira hadn't done a cold buffet.

Mark, she told him, out of choice, would not be present. He had opted to spend the evening with a friend.

The evening was comfortable, the way it is between old friends who like and respect each other. Naturally, with the occupations of the two men overlapping, the conversation occasionally turned to work.

'No further forward with your vagrant?' the Doc inquired while Moira and Shirley were washing up. 'I wouldn't say no,' he continued as Ian raised the whisky bottle in a silent question. 'And no need to stint. Shirley's driving.'

'When isn't she?' Ian said with affection rather than disapproval. 'And no, no further forward. But one or two other things are starting to move. I think we'll get there in the end. Problem is, our main suspect's gone walkabouts.'

'You have a suspect? That's something. Local man?'

'Yes. Rich local man. At least the wife is.' And then he stopped. Why hadn't he thought of it sooner? They knew from what Madelaine Chambers had said that her husband was a member of the Elms Golf and Country Club. The Doc must know him. As it was in the line of the investigation, it would be all right to discuss it with him. 'His name is Christopher Chambers.' He watched for the reaction and got the one he hoped for.

'Good God. Chambers?'

'How well do you know him?'

'Not intimately. Played a few rounds with him. Disappeared? When? I only saw him on Sunday.'

135

'Monday morning. He set off for work but never got there.'

'I should've been more persistent. There was obviously something deeply troubling him. I asked, but he wasn't saying what. He almost admitted he was desperate. I'm so sorry, Ian, I didn't realise. I assumed it was woman trouble.'

Moira and Shirley returned, bearing a tray of coffee, so the subject was dropped. Ian would have another chat with the Doc in the morning. There were limits as to how much of his job he could inflict on family and guests.

'One for the road?' he asked when the coffee was poured.

'Shirley?'

'Yes, go on, if you must,' his wife said, 'but I warn you, one of these days I'm going to get stinking drunk and you're going to have to carry me home.' They all smiled at the idea of the plump, pretty Shirley Harris ever being out of control.

'What time did Mark say he'd be home?' Ian asked when the Harrises had departed and Moira was washing the coffee cups and glasses.

'Eleven thirty. I know it's a school night, but he doesn't want to sit around listening to the likes of us. Don't frown, Ian, it's only ten past. What on earth would you be like if we had a daughter?'

It did not bear contemplation. He knew he would have to sit up every night until she came home.

'What time was he admitted?' the Chief asked when he was handed the message.

'A little after 4 a.m., sir.'

'Who informed us?'

'His wife. The hospital rang her. She rang us. We sent someone over to see her – she agreed to let us search without a warrant.'

Madelaine Chambers had seen no reason why Christopher's financial affairs should be called into question, but in her relief at knowing he was safe she had told the police officers they were free to look around. It seemed there was nothing suspicious in his monetary transactions. No large deposits or withdrawals had been made; there were only regular monthly payments and standing orders. Apart from one thing. Compared with the lifestyle the Chambers led it was a small sum, but it stood out on his latest bank statement because he rarely used cash and made very few withdrawals via the cash point machine. On the night of Charlie's death, however, he had done so, drawing one hundred pounds. Madelaine was unable to say why but thought it might be to spend on the woman she believed he was seeing. The Chief decided to think about it later.

'It's beginning to seem like home,' Barry commented sardonically as they circled the hospital car-park looking for a space. 'Are we arresting him?'

'Depends what he's got to say for himself. It's still difficult to prove anything.'

'Oh, come on, Ian, I'm not saying he drove the getaway lorry, or whatever, himself, but he must've been selling the information.'

'Well, let's ask him, shall we?'

'He was lucky,' the staff nurse told them. 'If it hadn't been for a patient on her way to maternity, he wouldn't have made it.'

'It was a genuine suicide attempt?'

'Definitely. This was no cry for help – they're usually satisfied with a handful of aspirins and a slug of alcohol, then they call an ambulance.'

137

'Can we see him?'

'Yes.' She nodded through the glass partition of her office. 'The bed just there.'

'Cynical young thing,' Barry commented as they made their way towards where Christopher Chambers lay. He was propped against the pillows, hardly recognisable from the carefree man in the snapshot. His complexion was grey and he seemed to have aged ten years, an illusion exaggerated by two days' growth of stubble and the dark circles beneath his eyes. His breathing was very shallow. The Chief studied him for a second or so, wondering if there was anything that would send him to the depths of despair, when he would contemplate taking his own life. He decided there wasn't.

A student nurse was tidying the bedclothes. 'Mr Chambers,' she said, 'you've got visitors.' Gently she shook his arm. He hardly stirred. She tried again. 'I don't think he's ready to talk yet. Why don't you come back later? We usually refer them to psychy after an overdose. Are you relatives?' The student nurse was curious; Sister didn't let many visitors in at this busy time of day.

'No, love, not relatives.' The Chief did not expound. She would know soon enough through hospital gossip.

'We may as well leave it for now,' he said to Barry. 'Staff'll keep a close eye on him. I'll get someone to sit with him.'

'They're not going to like it,' Barry said. 'The way we're going on we'll have an officer to every patient.'

'No. Hang on a minute.'

With the staff nurse's permission he rang Jenner Ward and asked to speak to the WPC on duty there.

'Yes, sir, if you're sure,' she said with relief in her voice when he told her she could return to the station. It was not the most exciting of jobs.

'Was that wise?' Barry wanted to know.

138

'I don't know what's wise any more. All I know is we've given her every opportunity to talk to us and she's still refusing to co-operate. We can't waste manpower watching her for ever and if she's unguarded it might make her think again. Oh, thanks, Staff, sorry about all this. We'll send someone along later to speak to Mr Chambers.'

She was more experienced than the student and knew better than to ask what her patient might have done.

'Before you go – Mr Whitten, one of our administrators, wants to see you. It's about Mr Chambers.'

The Chief glanced at the ward clock. It was a bit early for office staff to be on the premises.

'Where do we find him?'

She gave directions and they went to find him.

'He's probably had enough of us traipsing all over his hospital. Don't suppose it does the image much good.'

'It's not something I enjoy much either, Ian.'

The Chief smiled. He'd seen Barry's expression as they walked down the ward. He gazed steadfastly ahead, not liking to stare at people in their night-clothes, disliking even more the drip stands and machinery to which some were attached. Death and violence on the streets or in the mortuary were one thing: hospitals were a different matter. To Barry, like churches and cemeteries, they were a reminder of his own mortality.

'Come in,' Whitten said in response to their knock. 'I can't pretend I know what's going on here, but I thought it best to get in early. I'm sorry, do sit down.' But there were only two chairs. Whitten took the one behind the desk, the Chief took the other. Barry had to make do with resting his buttocks against the windowsill.

'Sister Gilbert rang me at home just after seven. She said a suicide had been admitted to her ward via casualty etc., and that the wife was informed immediately. Normal procedure, of course. Then she told me Mrs

139

Chambers was extremely upset and wanted her to call the police. Now I don't know what's going on, but it isn't doing the morale of the staff a lot of good having policemen all over the place. Mrs Chambers apparently insisted you be brought in. What exactly is he supposed to have done?'

'Mr Whitten, Mr Chambers may be able to help us clear up one or two things. We'd like to ask him some questions. What they concern, I'm afraid, is our business.' The Chief had taken an instant dislike to the man. His attitude was high-handed and his concern seemed only for the good name of the hospital rather than for the staff. He had not even inquired if Chambers was likely to be a danger to anyone.

'I see. Well, in that case, there's nothing more for me to do but to give you these.' He handed over two letters. One was addressed to the Chief, the other to Mrs Chambers.

'Why wasn't this given to Mrs Chambers at the time?'

'Because it was the ambulance driver who found them on the dashboard of Mr Chambers' car. Quite rightly, he handed them in to the casualty sister, Mr Chambers being unconscious at the time. They were placed in a sealed envelope and put in the safe until there was an appropriate time to deal with them. The patient's welfare comes first, Chief Inspector. I thought it best to hold on to them until a senior officer arrived.'

'I see.' It was not very flattering for the PC who had initially attended. 'You say they were found in Mr Chambers' car. Do you know exactly what happened?'

'More or less. A woman who lives in one of the outlying villages went into early labour. Her husband was driving her in to maternity when they saw a car parked off the road under some trees. Despite the wife's condition, she was certain she saw someone slumped over the steering wheel. The man stopped to confirm it

140

but due to the frequency of the labour pains, had to come straight on here. They rang for an ambulance from their mobile phone. Another lucky coincidence for Mr Chambers. They'd only recently acquired it because of the wife's condition and their isolated surroundings.'

'Thank you, Mr Whitten. We'll be sending someone along to speak to Mr Chambers, but you'll be pleased to know our WPC is no longer on Jenner Ward.'

'I'm beginning to stink of antiseptic,' Barry complained as they got into the car.

The Chief sat thoughtfully in the passenger seat.

'Aren't you going to open it?'

'What?'

'The letter.'

'He didn't leave the area after all. And Whitten was right. If Chambers parked up where I think he means, he was lucky to be found at all. Only farm traffic uses that road.' Although the town itself had spread, there were still many rural areas with large gaps between civilisation. 'Come on, let's get going.'

Barry pulled away and the Chief carefully opened the envelope addressed to himself. The second one had to be delivered to Madelaine Chambers. She would be asked to read it before it was handed over in evidence. If it was evidence.

'What does it say?'

'Watch the road, will you?'

Back in his office the Chief asked Barry to take a couple of copies for the file. 'I'll ring Mrs Chambers. If she hasn't gone back to the hospital, we'll go and see her right away. Send someone over to Rickenham General to arrest Chambers. And tell whoever it is to make sure he's wide awake and knows what's going on. We don't want him claiming he was forced into anything.'

The Chief had time for a quick cup of coffee while Barry made the necessary arrangements. As soon as they were completed they paid a visit to Madelaine Chambers.

High Elms Grange, like the golf club, was named after the beautiful trees which had once graced the landscape. Dutch elm disease had wiped them out but there were more than enough other varieties to ensure privacy. The Grange was situated on the edge of town but not too far out to be inconvenient. The outbuildings had been sold off to make small private residences, but it retained plentiful grounds. At the top of the drive stood the large detached house in front of which was the balustrade where Christopher Chambers had posed for his picture. Now the urns held evergreen ivies and miniature conifers. Only hard-pruned, thorny branches could be seen in the old-fashioned rose garden in the centre of the lawn.

Madelaine Chambers answered the door herself. Despite her lack of sleep and tell-tale signs of crying, she was still a striking woman. Dressed in a full-length emerald kimono with an exotic dragon snaking across one shoulder and down the back, she did not, as other women do when faced at such a disadvantage, pull the robe tighter or clasp it at the neckline. The Chief realised he was dealing with a woman confident in her body and her brain. There was a hint of cleavage and a flash of thigh as she turned to show them into a large, brightly decorated room to the right of the entrance hall. The entrance hall was almost a room in itself.

'You've seen him?' she asked, passing her hand across her forehead in a weary gesture. 'He looks absolutely dreadful.' She bowed her head and felt in her pocket for a tissue. 'I wish I knew what was going on.'

'We haven't been able to speak to your husband yet, Mrs Chambers. The reason we're here is that he left a letter for you. It was meant to be read . . . well, we'd like you to read it now, if you wouldn't mind.'

142

'It's all right, Chief Inspector, there's no need to protect me. You were going to say after he was dead.'

He handed her the envelope. 'I also had a letter. I'd like you to read yours and then I have to ask if you'd let me see it. You can read it in privacy if you wish.'

She took the letter, her hand only shaking slightly, and walked over to the writing desk against the wall. She did not tear open the envelope but picked up a letter knife and slit it carefully as if it were no more than the electricity bill. The Chief could only guess how much self-control she was exhibiting.

She read the first page with no sign of emotion; only when she turned over did her hand fly to her throat. She made a choking sound but no tears flowed. She sank into a soft armchair at one side of the fireplace. 'Oh, God,' she said. 'He really loved me. I didn't know. I really didn't know.'

The Chief and Barry exchanged glances. Was that all the letter said? Soon they would see for themselves but she needed a chance to recover from whatever she'd learned.

'I was right. There was another woman, but it wasn't what I thought. Oh, how could I have been so stupid?'

'May I see the letter, Mrs Chambers?' the Chief asked gently.

She nodded. As he reached to take it from her she began to tremble. 'It's my fault. All of it.'

He nodded towards the drinks tray. Barry went across and selected a bottle of brandy and took an upturned glass from the shelf beneath.

'No,' she said, 'I don't touch spirits. Only wine.'

Barry did not think red wine was ideal for the situation, but if that's what the lady wanted he would pour it for her.

'Please, have a drink yourselves. My mother, you see . . .' She stopped. Even after all these years she could not bring herself to admit the shame and disgust she felt for her mother, whose drinking habits had either led to her father's violence or been precipitated by it. Madelaine Chambers had escaped that dreadful childhood and never wanted to remember it. She had been beautiful and intelligent enough to marry well, but it was fondness she had felt for her first husband, not love. His death was a tragedy but she recovered. Later she met Christopher and they, too, married.

'I never told him I loved him, you see. I thought he knew. And the separate bedrooms, that was only because I suffer from insomnia. I didn't want to disturb him. He had to go to work.' Barry handed her the wine but she did not sip it. As she talked the Chief read her letter.

'I vowed', she said inconsequentially, 'never to touch spirits. I've seen what they can do to a person. You can become a slave to alcohol, by drinking too much or being afraid to touch it at all.' She studied her glass, wondering if it was a wise decision after all to touch it so early in the day. 'I'm sorry, I don't know why I'm going on like this.' She brushed back a tear angrily. 'It's of no interest to you.'

But it was, in a way. The Chief was always interested in the reasons behind people's behaviour. Even by the little she said he could guess at the sort of upbringing she'd had and that from an early age she probably learned it was safer not to show any emotions. She was only telling them now because they were strangers whom she'd hopefully never see again and she was at a stage in her life when she needed desperately to talk to someone.

'He's going to be all right, that's the main thing. The hospital sent me home to rest. It was no good. How can I when he's lying there? I must get dressed and go back.'

'Mrs Chambers, none of this has been easy for you,

144

but I feel it's only fair to tell you, we're placing your husband under arrest.'

'I see.' She bit hard on her lower lip, still fighting back the tears. 'And the charge will be . . . will be murder?'

That was a good question. 'Not necessarily,' was the best the Chief could come up with.

'But I don't understand. He says . . .'

'I know what the letter says, but there are several other factors to take into account. I can't say any more than that at the moment. Do you need a lift to the hospital?'

'No. Thank you. I'll have a shower first, make myself more presentable.'

'How could he, with a wife like that?' Barry asked after they left.

'Looks aren't everything, as you well know. Look, first you say you don't blame Wainright for going over the side, now you can't understand why Chambers did.'

'Yeah, but Mrs Wainright's like the back end of a bus.'

'No. It's not just that. Both men were unhappy because they couldn't get what they wanted at home. You've met both couples. It's obvious they don't talk to each other. If they did, none of this might have happened.'

'Do you talk to Moira? Well, I know you do, but about your sexual relationship?'

The Chief, once more in the passenger seat, fiddled with his seat belt.

'We don't need to, not after nineteen years.' He was not a man to discuss his bedtime or any other habits with colleagues.

'But you still do it, don't you?'

He frowned. 'Let's leave my private life out of this.' He knew he was being set up.

'Don't like to talk about it? And you going on about other people's lack of communication. Come on, you can

145

tell me, we've been together a long time. I'm the next best thing to a wife you'll ever have.'

The Chief laughed. 'Okay. And yes, we still do it, as you succinctly put it, but I'm not prepared to tell you exactly what we get up to.'

The smirk playing around the corners of his mouth intrigued Barry. He drove the rest of the way in silence. Despite his past reputation for womanising he was conjecturing whether there was something he didn't know about.

'We've talked to her, sir,' DC Campbell informed him. 'It was the right name and address. She's got a couple of young kids. It seems she thought she'd got it made. I got the impression she was ready to step into Mrs Chambers' shoes at the drop of a hat. The thing is, it was not quite what it seemed.'

'Oh?'

'Not the usual sort of bit on the side.'

'Don't keep it to yourself, Campbell.'

'The woman, Mary Gilbert, is divorced and she likes a good time. Her sister babysits so's she can get out at night. She goes out with friends to pubs and clubs, but that's not where she met Chambers. Now, this will interest you.'

'I'm sure it will – get on with it, for heaven's sake.'

'She came across a man named Alex Chambers. They got talking. Two of a kind, I'd imagine. Anyway, Alex makes her a proposition, one in which she can't lose. He wants her to make a play for his cousin. Now he doesn't say why, just that he'll pay her to be seen with him; if she has sex with him, better still. Even if it doesn't work she's guaranteed fifty per cent of the money.'

'How much?'

'A hundred quid.'

'Jesus. So how did this come about?'

'Alex rings his cousin and says he's in town and that

he wants to speak to him. They arrange a convenient place and time and Alex Chambers makes sure Mary Gilbert is also there. He introduces them, pretending the whole thing is just a social occasion, then leaves them to it. If you saw this woman you'd realise it must have been tempting.'

'Okay. So Alex has set Christopher up. But for what purpose?'

'She doesn't know. She went along with it to start with, just for the money. Once she realised the sort of lifestyle she might have if things became more serious, she set out to win Chambers.'

'And she voluntered all this information? Doesn't exactly put her in a good light, does it?'

'I happened to mention we were conducting a murder inquiry.'

'Ah. How did she take that piece of news?'

'Quite calmly. She was ready to tell us anything and everything as long as it got her off the hook. I think she put all thought of a future with Christopher Chambers out of her mind there and then.'

'Thanks, Alan. Carry on the search for Alex Chambers.'

'Yes, sir.' DC Alan Campbell left the room with a smile. It was the first time the Chief had called him by his Christian name.

12

Having read Mary Gilbert's typed statement, the Chief believed she knew nothing whatever of his criminal activities. As far as she was concerned, he was her lover. She came across as being not very intelligent, and certainly not very curious if she did not bother to ask why Alex Chambers wanted her to seduce his cousin.

'So,' he said to himself after he had reread the letter addressed to himself, 'now we know who didn't kill Charlie, we'd better concentrate on finding out who did.' But first he had to make an interim report to Superintendent Thorne.

'I do wish you'd drop the "sir" when we're alone, Ian. It's rather offputting.'

'Sorry, s . . . Michael.' But it did not run easily off the tongue. Old habits die hard. Ross had insisted on being addressed formally at all times.

Michael Thorne spotted the difficulty. 'Try Mike,' he said, his Birmingham accent altering the vowel.

'All right, Mike it is.'

'I hear you've got a written admission.'

'Yes. But first I'll fill you in on some relevant facts. Christopher Chambers is married to a beautiful and wealthy woman. He's got it made, you might think. Unfortunately his wife is unable to show her feelings. It transpires that she does love him but he's probably unaware of it. Christopher has a cousin, Alex. Known to the Met, by the way – no convictions, but it's only a matter of time. He's short of cash. He knows his cousin's occupation and his marital position and uses this knowledge to set him up. He comes across a female who won't say no to some extra cash herself and gets her to seduce him.'

'Just like that.'

'I needn't go into the details but don't forget, Christopher Chambers is crying out for some affection. He probably wouldn't have gone looking for it, but when it's handed to you on a plate, well . . .'

'All right, Ian, I get your drift.'

'Alex Chambers now has him exactly where he wants him. We've only got Christopher's word for it, but Alex threatens to tell Madelaine what's been going on – and, naturally, he has photographic proof – unless Christopher provides certain information concerning properties which Alex is interested in. He wants to know where certain goods may be found and the details of the alarm and security systems.'

'So no money changes hands.'

'No. The only price Alex is prepared to pay is silence.'

'Why didn't he tell him to get lost, or admit it to his wife himself?'

'That we don't know yet, but I suspect he was aware of Mrs Chambers' miserable early life and wanted to spare her any more pain. He says it was a stupid mistake, that he didn't love Gilbert, but once he was in he managed to get in even deeper.'

'How come?'

'He decides he's had enough. He lets Mary Gilbert know her cards are marked and asks to meet Alex to tell him to do his worst. At the same time he changes jobs, hoping both to avoid detection and to fool Alex into thinking he no longer has access to the information he wants.'

'Excuse me, Ian, what part does Alex Chambers play in this?'

'Ah, that's where he's clever. He sells on the information, or at least, that's how it appears. So he's never at the scene of a crime and he doesn't have to wait until it's committed to get his cut.'

'And in this instance it's a hundred per cent profit because he doesn't even have to pay his cousin.'

'Exactly. But things don't work out as Christopher hopes. He settles into his new job but Alex won't let go of the golden goose. He arranges to meet him one last time. He chooses a pub called the Prince William. It's a back-street pub, one not frequented by the likes of Christopher Chambers.'

'Only by the likes of Markham?' Thorne was grinning. There wasn't much he didn't know about the men under him.

'Er, well, yes. Whilst they're there, Alex makes his first mistake. He doesn't realise that the conversation relating to the JC Warehousing robbery is overheard by a grubby little man called George Miller. Miller thinks there's a cheap video to be had and, having the hide of a rhinoceros, butts in and says he's willing to buy one. Now Alex, being a clever little bastard, turns this to his advantage. Here he is with a witness to prove Christopher is involved. Once more Christopher is back in his power.'

'How does he go about this?'

'Alex makes a phone call, then he disappears. All three then go in Alex's car to the flats where Miller lives. There, in the doorway, Alex hands him the video, Miller hands him the cash.'

'Hang on, Ian, how come he gets his hands on one so easily? I felt sure they must all be out of the area. We've not heard a squeak about any others.'

'We don't know that yet. Anyway, despite all this,

150

Christopher still insists he wants out. Alex finally has to agree. He knows his man well enough to realise that if he pushed it much further he might just give the whole thing away. But then we have Charlie.'

'I wondered when you were coming to that.'

'Charlie is insignificant. A dirty old tramp, probably half mad or drunk or both. If Alex and Christopher even saw him I doubt they'd've taken much notice of his presence. But in fact he is none of these things. He sees the whole transaction. Then one evening he spots Christopher coming out of his office and takes a chance. Christopher, in his statement, says he can't remember exactly what Charlie said to him other than that it was to do with videos and how about a little extra for keeping his mouth shut.'

'The man needs a psychiatrist, falling for blackmail a second time.'

'He'll be seeing one now. But you have to understand his state of mind. Just when he thinks he's off the hook and maybe life can get back to normal, along comes Charlie. Now, Charlie isn't stupid either. He only asks for a tenner, hoping he can keep going back. The following week he's had time to think about it and demands twenty.'

'That was the night Chambers withdrew a hundred from the cash point?'

'Yes. He had it in mind to pay Charlie off with one lump sum. It was the act of a desperate man: black-mailers don't work like that.'

'But he changed his mind when he saw him.'

'Yes. He gave him the twenty and arranged to see him later. Obviously he didn't want to be seen negotiating with him in St Hilda's Walk. When he gets there Charlie is sitting against the fence. It's pitch dark down there and all Chambers can see is his man leaning casually against the fence. He bends down to speak to him and it appears that Charlie, whose eyes were half open, is sneering at him. That's when something snapped. Don't forget this all happened in a matter of seconds. There's no one around, he picks up the nearest thing to hand, which happens to be the brick, and whacks him. He claims it was only meant as a warning, to show he wasn't having it.'

'How come he wasn't questioned along with the other office workers?'

'He's out of the office mostly. The first he knew of Charlie's death was when he read about it in the *Rickenham Herald*. We deliberately left out the cause of death so he assumes he's killed him. It takes Chambers the whole weekend to decide what to do. Doc Harris can confirm the sort of state he was in.'

'But suicide?'

'He said he thought it was better for Madelaine that way.'

'Well done, Ian. But we're no closer to tracing the stolen goods or finding Charlie's real killer.'

'What gets me, though, is still not knowing who Charlie was.'

'We may never know. Content yourself with finding his murderer.'

George Miller was sitting miserably in the interview room when Ian came back from making his report. He was wearing the ubiquitous coat and scarf and seemed to have a cold. Now and then he produced a soiled cotton handkerchief from his pocket and ineffectually wiped his nose.

'I've told you everything,' he repeated to DC Winston Emmanuel who was handling the interview, 'just like I told that other one.'

152

'Not quite everything. How about your being escorted home? How about the tramp, the one that was killed?'

There was naked fear in Miller's eyes. His voice was high when he said, 'You don't think I did it?'

'I don't need to think, Mr Miller, not when I've got you here to tell me. What do you know about Charlie?'

'Nothing.'

'You've never set eyes on him in your life, I suppose.'

'I never said that.'

'Oh?'

'I may have seen him.' Winston sat back. Those three little words. I may have. I might have been. What if I was? They all meant the same thing. An affirmative.

'And when do you think you might've seen him?'

'Here and there.'

'Here? In the station?'

'You know what I mean.'

'I don't, Mr Miller, that's why I'm asking.'

'All right. Outside the flats sometimes. I've never even spoken to him. I wouldn't, not someone like that.' Winston let that one go. Miller was no pin-up himself. 'He'd go through the dustbins sometimes. I don't like to speak ill of the dead, but he was disgusting.'

Winston recalled some distant school poetry, something about seeing ourselves as others see us, but doubted if Miller would appreciate the reference.

Eventually and begrudgingly Miller signed a statement to the effect that he had purchased the video from two men – one he only knew as Alex; the other he didn't know at all by name but was able to identify from the photograph of Christopher Chambers.

That was as far as they could go that day. The Chief rounded up a few of his colleagues and they headed for the pub.

One or two shop windows were already displaying

Christmas stock. The usual comments about the season starting earlier each year were made as they struggled against the wind. Screwed-up fish and chip paper hit Barry in the leg as it was lifted into the air in the slipstream of a passing bus. He kicked it away disdainfully. The serious littering would come later, the take-away cartons and wrappers from the kebabs served from a caravan by the bus station. After an evening's drinking even the glutinous mess that found its way between the pitta bread seemed appetising.

'What's it to be, gentlemen?' the landlord of the Three Feathers inquired, knowing who his customers were and grateful for some early evening trade.

'Lager,' Markham grunted as he placed two pound coins on the counter, making it clear he was not drinking in rounds. No one expected otherwise.

They found a corner seat with room to accommodate them all and talked and smoked and sipped their drinks, discussing cases past and present. Once work was out of their systems, the conversation turned to Christmas and the CID do. As their wives and girlfriends could attest, the police knew how to entertain. The venue was chosen by the higher-ups but once a ticket was purchased the food and drink were free and the music loud. It was an event which was anticipated with an equal mixture of pleasure and dread. There was always the question of who would disgrace themselves this year. Whose wife might over-indulge and vomit down the Super's trousers. Ian could never understand why Moira enjoyed it so much; given the choice, he'd have done away with the whole thing.

'One more before we go?' Winston Emmanuel offered.

'Take it easy,' Barry told him. 'I'm only half-way down this one.'

'Chief? Can I get you one?' Ian looked dubiously at his glass. There was an inch left in it. 'Go on,' Winston encouraged. 'It'll give the missus time to slip into something comfortable.'

'Don't you ever think about anything else? All right. You've talked me into it.'

It had taken far more door-knocking than expected to locate the whereabouts of Alex Chambers. Hotels and listed guest and boarding houses were easy: they could be checked by telephone from the station. He was at none of them. However, the job was made a little easier because he had used his own name. Markham had been able to tell them that from the first time he saw the man.

It was then a matter of checking bed and breakfast accommodation, making inquiries in newsagents and sub-post offices where vacant rooms were advertised in the window. At last they struck lucky.

'Mrs Beard took someone in. Yes, now you come to mention it, his name is Alex. She's always saying what a pleasant man he is, and clean too. You wouldn't believe what some of them can be like.' The PC took down the address, left the shop and radioed the information back to headquarters. DS Markham and DC Campbell went along to pick him up.

Alex Chambers' landlady showed them in. 'He's not here. He left a couple of days ago. I'll show you his room if you like.'

They followed her up the stairs. 'Did he say where he was going or leave a forwarding address?' Markham asked.

'No. And it wasn't my business to ask, was it, love?'

Markham said nothing but would have bet a month's salary she had.

'Pity he had to go. Such a nice, comfortable man. Clean and tidy. I could tell you tales about some of them. Here we are, this was his room.' She smoothed her tight skirt over generous hips as if in remembrance of other occasions in that room. 'It's not bad news, I hope? As I said, such a pleasant man.'

Markham and Campbell, although not usually on each other's wavelength, were thinking the same thing: just how pleasant had Alex Chambers been to this hopeful divorcee?

'No, not bad news. Just a couple of things we wanted to ask him.'

'You want to question Alex? I can't believe it. What's he done?'

Markham sighed. Why did everyone assume that if someone was questioned they were automatically guilty? Of course, in this case the woman was right.

Overseen by the landlady they opened the wardrobe and looked in the drawers. Chambers had left nothing behind. The bed was already made up with clean linen. He might never have been there.

'You won't find anything. Like I told you, I always give the rooms a good clean and an airing the minute my guests leave.'

'Are you sure he didn't give you any idea of where he was going?'

'No. He wasn't here all that long, and he never got any post. He's got a London accent though. Probably gone back there.'

'Well, if you should think of anything that'll help us find him, give us a ring, would you?'

She took the card Markham handed her and glanced at it. The look she gave Markham suggested she might just ring the number anyway.

At the door she tried to detain them with small talk, hoping her neighbours were watching. Later she would regale them with tales of how she had harboured a dangerous criminal, how all the time he'd been under her roof she'd known there was something not quite right about him.

'I wouldn't be surprised if she's right, if he has gone back to London,' Campbell said. 'Easier to lose himself there.'

Alex had not disappeared because he was aware that they were on to him. It was the instinct of a streetwise villain. His cousin was of no further use to him, therefore there was no longer any point in staying.

Sheila Dixon walked confidently into the George. This was one of Mandy's haunts but as Mandy was out of action she would try it herself.

Despite the beams and the red plush and the horse brasses it was not an old building. The general mock effect might grate on the nerves of the more discerning but it did have some advantages. There was no pool table and no juke-box and the prices, although high, were set to discourage the rougher element. The clientele consisted mostly of businessmen who came in for a decent steak lunch or dinner: although the drinks were pricey, the food was good value. The classical music playing quietly in the background lent the place an air of being something better than it really was.

Here, men came straight from work to relax over a couple of drinks and read the paper. It was in the bar of the George that Mandy Philpotts also plied her trade, but so discreetly it was not known to the management.

Sheila surveyed the room as she crossed to the bar. The barman, neat in short-sleeved white shirt and bow-tie, asked what she wanted. 'Vodka and Coke, please,' she said. He poured the drink and took her money. Aware that he was watching her in the mirror behind the bar she asked if the clock was right. 'My watch has stopped and I'm meeting someone. I thought I might be late.'

She took herself to a corner of the room. It was more reminiscent of a hotel lounge than a bar. Sheila was not unaware of the glances she was receiving but ignored them. As she had told the barman she was meeting someone, it was too soon to make a move. She sipped her drink and, from time to time, looked at the clock. After fifteen minutes or so a man who had been sitting at a low table, briefcase open in front of him as he studied some papers, stood up and came across, ostensibly on his way to the toilets. He smiled, and upon receiving an answering one said, 'I couldn't help overhearing what you said at the bar. Do you think your friend's going to turn up?'

'It doesn't look like it now. Never mind. I could do with an early night.'

'It seems a shame to waste the evening now you're here. Look, I'll just . . .' he indicated the door of the gents' toilets, 'then perhaps you'd let me buy you a drink?'

Sheila hesitated. 'Well, all right, if you're sure.' This was new territory but it had not proved to be a problem.

The man, whose name was Phillip, bought several drinks, large ones for Sheila. They chatted, passing the time until the inevitable conclusion. Naturally, he offered to give her a lift home. Naturally, she accepted. Only when they pulled into a gateway a couple of miles out of town on the Saxborough Road did the trouble start. Sheila asked him for money up front.

'You little slut,' Phillip spat at her, 'you dirty little slut.'

'What did you expect? You said you were married. And you're no great looker. I suppose you think it's all right for . . .' but she got no further. The crack of his hand as he slapped her across the face silenced her.

'I've never had to pay for sex. Never.'

He hit her again. Sheila struggled to get the car door open and landed in the muddy earth, rutted with tractor wheels, because her foot was caught in the seat belt. Phillip slammed the door shut behind her, revved up the engine, swung round in the road and headed back towards Rickenham Green.

'You bastard,' she shouted after the departing car. It would take a good forty-five minutes to walk back and there would be no other business forthcoming tonight, not as she was, plastered in mud. And there was Vic to meet.

At eleven thirty the shrill ringing of the telephone caused Ian to knock half a mug of cold tea off the arm of his chair. He had fallen asleep in front of the television. He swore, promising he would replace the telephone with a push-button handset which purred gently instead of setting his nerves jangling.

'Sorry to disturb you, sir, but we've got Sheila Dixon here wanting to make a statement.'

The machinery of his brain took a second or two to shake off the after-effects of sleep. Sheila Dixon was? Ah, yes, Mandy Philpotts' flatmate.

'Okay. I'm on my way.'

'Ian?' Moira appeared at the top of the stairs.

'Sorry, love, I've got to go in. This might be the break we're looking for. I'll try not to wake you.'

But she knew he would. Like his son, Ian found it difficult to do anything quietly. 'See you later,' she said and went back to bed.

Ian dutifully mopped up the tea before he left.

'She's in Interview Room 3, sir. Says she's not leaving without protection. WPC Davies is with her. I'm surprised she didn't go to the hospital.'

'Ah, Ian, seems none of us is allowed to rest in the bosom of our families for long.'

'Hello, Doc. What's brought you here?'

'Your case, I believe, the Dixon girl.'

'Hurt?'

'Quite a bit. But she's a tough one. She'll live. Must go. Shirley's waiting up.'

Ian took a deep breath and went in to see what Sheila Dixon had to say.

In the chair sat what should have been a very pretty girl. But sourness and an expression of having seen it all marred her looks. Her mouth was bleeding and one eyelid was beginning to swell, otherwise she appeared unhurt.

'Hello, Sheila, I'm Chief Inspector Roper. I believe you have something to say to me.'

'I do. But I'm not leaving here, not until you've got him behind bars. It's a pity Mandy didn't tell you.'

'Perhaps you'd better start at the beginning.'

Sheila related the scene in the car. 'All right, you'll find out at some time. I asked him for money. That's why he hit me. I don't usually make a mistake, he seemed all right.'

'Did you get his registration number?'

'No.' But she had. She always did. But it wasn't Phillip she wanted behind bars.

'Look, I understand what you're telling me. There's nothing I can charge you with and unless you want to press charges against this man, you're wasting my time. I could do with some sleep. No doubt you could too. I'll get someone to drive you home.'

'No. I can't go back there. He'll kill me.'

'Who'll kill you, Sheila? I thought you said this man was married. He'll be safely back with his wife now.' Ian lit a cigarette and leant back in his chair. He saw by the way her face crumpled that there was more to come.

160

Sheila Dixon fished in her own handbag and produced a packet of cigarettes. She looked up as if seeking permission to smoke one. Ian nodded and offered her a light.

'Look at this, ' she said, unexpectedly standing up and lifting up her top. She had no false modesty, she was used to men staring at her body. Her ribcage was already red. Ian could see that later there would be extensive bruising. Sheila Dixon was hard all right. She must have been in considerable pain. But her fear of some unknown man was the uppermost thing in her mind.

'It was Vic,' she said. 'He did this to me, and this.' She held her long, blonde hair back and showed him her ear. An ear-ring had been torn out, splitting the lobe. 'And it was Vic who did that to Mandy.'

'Vic.' Ian doodled on a pad on the table in front of him waiting for some further explanation.

'I, we, work for him. The three of us.'

'Would you care to elucidate?'

'Do I have to spell it out?' She puffed furiously on the stub of her cigarette before squashing it out in the ashtray and immediately lighting another one.

'I used to be an actress, I was never out of work until I got to about seventeen. I couldn't get parts playing children any longer but no one would give me a chance as an adult.' She sighed. 'The man who produced the last thing I was in promised me television work. Well, you can guess the rest. I went to his place to audition but I never got the work. He wasn't the only one either. I decided if that was what I was reduced to I wasn't going to do it for nothing.'

'What's any of this got to do with Vic?'

'I met a girl just over from Ireland. We got together, shared digs and tried to make ourselves some money. Vic got to hear about it. He lived in the same neighbourhood. He wanted his cut.'

161

'So Vic's your pimp.'

He saw the distaste when he used the word. 'I suppose you could say that.'

'But why come here? It's a far cry from the Smoke.'

'He was in some sort of trouble. I don't know what. He said he'd got contacts here.'

'Contacts?'

'It's no good asking me. He never told us anything. Contacts is all I know.'

'Are you telling me, Sheila, that this man, Vic, is running some sort of brothel here?'

She smiled wryly. 'Are you telling me, Chief Inspector, that you didn't know?'

Touché, he thought, lighting another cigarette himself. He avoided the eye of the officer responsible for the recording equipment.

'It's not a brothel,' she conceded. 'None of us has ever worked from the flat.'

'How does it work then?'

'We go to places where we're likely to find suitable clients. Businessmen, mostly. People who won't talk. But mostly it's by prior arrangement. Vic knows a lot of people. We use hotels out of the town. Some of them are quite happy in the back of the car.'

'Very salubrious. You can spare me the grisly details. What you're saying is that you have regular clients.'

'Yes.'

'And if Vic has made the arrangements he knows exactly what they pay you. What do you get out of it?'

'Twenty-five per cent.'

'Is it worth it?'

'You'd be surprised. And free accommodation.'

Ah. Now that was more interesting. They were living in Wainright's property. No doubt he'd been able to suggest a few names to Vic. 'Free accommodation? How come?'

162

'I don't know. All Vic said was that he'd seen an ad for a house to let and had answered it. The man concerned was prepared to let him have it for nothing in return for our services whenever he wanted.' That, at least, confirmed Wainright's story.

'And Mandy? Was it true how you met her?'

'Yes. I was waiting for Vic one night at the arranged place and she was there. She looked so lost. It was just like we said in our statements.'

Ian avoided using the expression 'tart with a heart of gold', but was this a real coincidence, that Mandy just happened to be there? 'And what did Vic have to say about you taking in someone else?'

'He was all right about it. He took her out a couple of times. Next thing we knew, she was working with us. He can be a charming bastard when he puts his mind to it. He'd easily have talked her into it.'

'And she went along with it that easily? Could it be that there's still something you're not telling me, Sheila? Like she agreed to work for him if he kept her supplied with drugs?'

'No.' But Ian knew she was lying.

'All right, Sheila. Thanks for popping in. You can get your coat and go now.'

'No. Wait.'

Ian was standing, his hand on the door handle. 'Yes?'

'We didn't know. Honestly. Not at first. Marie and I don't take them and we didn't realise Mandy did, not for some time. Not until she admitted herself to hospital that night.'

'And the second time, when Vic beat her?'

'We were there, Marie and me. Vic never came to the house, that was an exception. Mandy let him in. He said he wanted a quiet word with her. We went to our room.'

'And when you heard her scream you stayed in your room?'

163

Sheila nodded. 'Don't think we're proud of the fact, but what else could we do? Next time it would be one of us.'

'Yes. Very courageous. What had Mandy done to deserve it in Vic's eyes?'

'She'd hinted on and off that she didn't want to work for him any more. He said he would stop her rations.'

'Of drugs?' He wanted it clear.

'Yes.'

'And did he?'

'I don't know. But the night he came to the flat I heard some of the conversation. Mandy had been doing a bit of freelance work, not handing over the money. Vic found out about it.'

'I think that'll do for now. But Sheila, I need Vic's surname.'

'Marsh. Vic Marsh. Don't you want to know why he did this to me?'

'If you want to tell me.'

'Because of Mandy, because he didn't believe me when I said I hadn't earned anything tonight. God, you'd think he could see by the state of me I was telling the truth. But no, he got it into his head that we were all at it. I can't go back there. You'll have to keep me here.'

'I don't have to do any such thing, Sheila. And what about Marie? Don't you have any concern for her safety?'

'Marie's all right. As soon as she realised it was happening again she legged it. I don't know where she's gone, but I don't think she'll ever show her face at the flat again.'

'If we find Victor Marsh, are you prepared to go to court and repeat what you've told me tonight?'

'Yes. I am. But Mandy won't press charges.'

'She doesn't need to. We can get him on a drugs offence.' Hopefully, Ian reminded himself. 'It's probably

164

a stupid question, but you don't happen to have his address, do you?'

'No. Do you think I wouldn't have told you if I did?'

He believed her. 'Look, I'll see what I can do. I can't promise anything, though. Do you have any money on you?'

'About twenty pounds.'

'You stay here. I'll get some tea sent up. Are you sure you don't want to go to the hospital?'

She grinned and her face altered. 'They won't keep me in.'

'I get your point.'

The best he could come up with was cheap bed and breakfast for which Sheila agreed to pay.

'Thanks,' she said as she was escorted out to a waiting car, 'but God knows what I'll do tomorrow.'

'Victor Marsh,' the Chief said, tapping his teeth thoughtfully with a pen. 'The name doesn't ring any bells.'

'Nor with me,' Barry admitted, stifling a yawn. It felt like the middle of the night. 'But someone must know him.' He read the description given by Sheila Dixon. 'Can't say this means anything either. Shouldn't be too hard to find, not with tattoos all over his knuckles. Where do we start looking?'

'I'm going to leave that to you, Barry, but I suggest you start with anyone known to be associated with drugs.'

'What are you going to do?'

'Find Charlie's killer.'

The Chief read through Christopher Chambers' long and detailed statement again. He had left nothing out, find-

165

ing it a great relief to be able to tell someone. When he finally signed it and was told that he was not responsible for Charlie's death, it hardly seemed to matter. The only thing that concerned him was that Madelaine had made her feelings plain. Awkwardly and shyly, but nonetheless honestly. And she was going to stand by him. Ironically, considering the situation which he was in, he now believed himself to be the luckiest man in the world.

He had not remained in hospital long and had agreed to everything and anything suggested to him, only grateful that he was to be allowed home with his wife. He was prepared to take whatever followed. All of it, the crime, the blackmail, the anxiety, those hours while he decided the best course to take, every minute was worth it if Madelaine was by his side.

One day he would try to explain about Mary Gilbert but not just yet. He wasn't even sure himself how that had come about.

He had been given a second chance. Christopher Chambers was not going to waste it.

13

Ian, having been called out late to interview Sheila
Dixon, had found when he returned home that his mind
was too active to allow him to sleep. He settled in his
armchair and tried to read but it was no use. At six thirty
he had returned to the station.

Unable to sleep, he saw no reason why anyone else
should either. At seven he'd rung Barry and asked him
to come in. He had delegated the job of finding Victor
Marsh but had not been strictly truthful when he said he
was going to work on Operation Charlie. What he was
actually going to do was go home and get a couple of
hours' sleep.

It was unusual for him to enter his own house when it
was completely empty but Mark was at school and Moira
had left for work. He made tea and toast and wrote a
note saying he was upstairs asleep in case she didn't
notice the car. His body, humped under the bedclothes,
might give her a nasty shock if she didn't realise he was
there.

Whilst Ian slept, Barry put into motion the search for
Victor Marsh. Once the pubs were opened questions
started there. Sheila Dixon had said Vic smoked. He had
to buy his cigarettes somewhere. The supermarkets were
cheaper but many people used the corner shop nearest

167

to them if they ran out. Someone, somewhere, had to recognise him.

Like Alex Chambers, Vic had made one mistake. Men like Vic, vain and arrogant, a bully with a high opinion of himself, believed they were outside the normal run of things. He earned a lot of money without having to lift a finger. He earned it through prostitution and he earned it by selling drugs. Men like Vic, who enjoyed the easy life, had their newspapers delivered.

'Must be the same one,' the newsagent told the PC who was making the inquiry. 'That's certainly his name. Always pays his bill on time, and yes, come to think of it, I'm sure he's got tattoos.' He gave the PC David Victor Marsh's address.

'Ian?' He didn't know where he was. He knew he was warm and comfortable but his eyelids felt gritty when he tried to open his eyes. Daylight was coming through the curtains and someone was standing over him shaking his arm.

'Moira? What's the matter?'

'Telephone.'

'Goddam it all. What time is it?'

She told him. He'd only been asleep a couple of hours. Deep sleep too. He had not heard her return or the telephone ringing.

Wearing only underpants and shirt, the clothes in which he'd gratefully slipped under the duvet, he stomped downstairs.

'Roper here. What is it?'

He listened for a few minutes then said, 'Hold him. No. I want to see him myself. I'll be in in about half an hour.'

Moira knew what that meant. He wanted coffee before

he went. 'Charlie's killer?' she asked as she put the kettle on.

'No. But something nearly as good. Put some sugar in that, will you? I need the energy.' For once she did as he asked. 'I'm getting too bloody old for these unsocial hours.' Moira ruffled his hair as she went to fetch it.

He had half a second cup then put on the rest of his clothes.

David Victor Marsh sat in an interview room, hands clasped loosely behind his head, his gaze fixed nonchalantly on the ceiling, apparently unconcerned about his arrest. It was explained to him how the interview was to be conducted and he was asked if he understood. He said he did. He agreed his name was as they said and that he lived at that address, but that was as far as he was prepared to comment.

'It's no good,' the Chief told him. 'We have witnesses who've already made statements.' Still no response. 'Look, we know you make a living from immoral earnings and you can also be charged with actual and grievous bodily harm. You may get a short custodial sentence; maybe the judge'll see fit to lock you up for a long time.'

Victor did no more than smile.

'However,' the Chief continued, 'that's small-time compared with dope peddling and murder.'

At last there was a flicker in Vic's eyes. Not so much fear as wariness. But he could no longer remain silent.

'Murder? What're you talking about?' It was interesting to note that he did not claim to know nothing about drugs.

'I think you know.'

'Mandy's not dead.' He had him now. Those three words gave it all away.

'Okay, Mr Marsh, shall we start again? Hold on.' He

169

turned to Barry. 'How long's he been here?' Barry told him. 'Do you want some tea or coffee?' Every so many hours detainees had to be offered refreshment.

Vic nodded. The Chief left the room and indicated that Barry was to come with him.

'Anything?' he asked when they were the other side of the door.

'Not so far. No local form. We're still waiting to hear from London.'

By the time the coffee arrived Vic was ready to talk.

'It can't be possible that Philpotts killed Charlie.'

'Why not? He'd a few drinks inside him, he's getting on and rage can give you extra strength.' But even as Ian spoke these words he knew he did not believe them. Philpotts was a nasty piece of work, she'd used everyone that crossed her path and she took drugs, but she had not killed Charlie.

'What about Danny Grant? Are we going to pick him up?'

'That's not our baby. Customs and Excise will see to that.'

'Do you think it's something bigger than what Marsh is telling us?'

'No. I'm sure it's a small operation. At least, I hope it is, otherwise we might be treading on the toes of the drugs squad. For all we know they might have someone under cover. Anyway, I'll speak to the relevant authorities, then we'll know.'

'I've had it up to here with females,' Ian said that evening as he watched Moira peeling vegetables. 'First this Philpotts girl, then Barry starts winding Judy Robbins up

170

and much as I love the girl, when her temper's roused I prefer not to be around.'

'He's probably had a row with Lucy,' Moira suggested correctly.

'Well, they should keep their personal lives for their own time.'

Moira said nothing. She knew Ian did not always practise what he preached.

'How long's that going to take? I'm bloody starving.'

This time Moira did respond. 'It works two ways, you know. You don't like it when people's personal lives overlap into work, I don't like it when you bring your bad temper back here. Now go and sit down with a beer, it won't be more than twenty minutes.'

Suitably chastened, Ian did as he was told. When she called him out to the kitchen to eat he apologised. 'I'm sorry, you're right. It's just so frustrating – two crimes, okay, serious crimes, cleared up, both seemingly con- nected with Charlie's murder, but we're no nearer solv- ing it. And what makes it worse, I think the people we've arrested are telling the truth.'

'Mind, the plate's hot.' Moira placed his meal in front of him, steam rising in appetising curls. 'I tell you what, we'll have this, then we'll go out for a quiet drink and you can get it off your chest. I can't stand it when you're like this, it gets my stomach in knots. And it can't do much for yours, you'll end up with an ulcer if you're not careful.'

Ian picked up his knife and fork. He was a little afraid of this new wife of his. Since she had started working she had changed in some imperceptible way. He couldn't exactly put his finger on it because nothing had really altered. The house was still spotless, meals were on time and their sex life remained satisfying. Perhaps it was because he was in his fifties, his career probably at its apex, whilst she was just finding her feet. There were times when those fifteen years made a lot of difference. Was he jealous? He thought about it as he chewed his lamb chop. No, she'd never really given him cause to be. In fact, he was rather proud of her.

'I'll just wash up,' she said when they finished, 'then we'll go. Mark's bringing Emma round, they'll be glad we're going out. I can remember what it was like the first time I met your parents. They thought you were cradle snatching.'

'Did they?'

'Ah, here they are. We're out here,' she called.

'Dad, this is Emma.' Mark was flushed with exertion, both from his tennis coaching and with apprehension. Mum was no problem. She was young and pretty and modern, but his father's ideas were sometimes a little old-fashioned. And it was always an embarrassment admitting how he earned his living.

Ian stood up and offered his hand. 'Hello, Emma, pleased to meet you.'

'And you, Mr Roper,' Emma replied, taking his hand. 'I've been looking forward to it. Mark's talked a lot about you and what you do.'

Mark shoved his hands in his pockets, trying to appear casual but wishing she had not said that. Emma, a year younger than Mark, was the more confident of the two. Ian had not known what to expect but not this girl who, although not classically beautiful, had a definite attraction. She was well built, her figure solid but shapely, and she dressed with flair, not in the baggy, androgynous clothes favoured by most teenagers. Her hair was dark, longer at the back than the sides and her face was all smiles. But it was the eyes which caught the attention. They were wide-spaced, greenish-grey and glistening. Ian looked at them, the one so fair, the other so dark, and an unbidden thought came into his head. He wondered which of them their children would favour.

'Come on, I'm ready,' Moira prompted when Emma and Mark had gone upstairs to listen to music.

'Are we walking?'

'Yes. Unless you want to drive,' Moira said, making it clear that she fancied a drink herself.

They walked close together and briskly up as far as the Plough. It was the nearest pub but not particularly favoured by either of them. However, they knew it would be quiet. It nearly always was.

Settled in a seat near the artificial log fire, Ian placed a dry white wine in front of Moira and his own pint on a beer-mat.

'Cheers. Now, do you want to tell me?'

Ian nodded. He had total trust in Moira's confidence. Nothing he ever told her went any further. How many policemen, or any men, could say that?

'Christopher Chambers', he began, 'tried to kill himself.' He explained how he had been trapped then blackmailed by his cousin, had managed to get out of that only to get into a similar position with Charlie.

'And he thought he'd killed him. The poor man. What he must've suffered.' Ian did not entirely go along with his wife's views. The man was a fool to get involved in the first place. 'But what's the warehouse robbery got to do with anything else?'

'We're still not certain. We have Mandy Philpotts, on drugs, gets beaten up. She's living in accommodation owned by Basil Wainright. Wainright uses her services, Wainright's involved with Victor Marsh.'

'Hold on, Ian, you're losing me already.'

Once more he stopped to explain the connection between the people involved.

'Right,' Moira said. 'Mandy and Danny – Grant is it? –

they leave London because Danny's trying to get into drugs in a big way and the locals don't like it.'

'Yes. One of the locals being Victor Marsh who thinks he's big-time but isn't. They need some breathing space and pick Felixstowe.'

'Why?'

'Fishing boats. Marsh has enough contacts to get Danny a job. Once they're out at sea they go about their legal business but before they return they meet up with another boat. Possibly French, we're not sure yet. They've got away with it simply because it's such a small operation.'

'Customs?'

'They don't cut open every individual fish.'

'So why's Marsh in Rickenham?'

'To distance himself. He's already got Marie O'Doyle and Sheila Dixon working for him. He's shrewd, is Marsh. He'd made inquiries about several properties but he spotted Wainright for what he is. A sleazebag. He used this fact to get the accommodation free. There's no paperwork, no rent book, nothing to tie him in if he decided to leg it. Now in return for cutting Danny in on the business he insists Mandy works for him. He sets it up that she meets Sheila so it appears her being here is pure chance. When he thinks Mandy's double-crossing him he puts her in hospital.'

'Nice boy.'

'Very. Well, we've got Christopher Chambers' confession, we've got people looking for Alex Chambers and when we have him we might discover where the rest of the missing goods have gone, and we've got a full confession from Victor Marsh.'

'I still can't see it. What makes you so sure all these things revolve around each other?'

'Marsh's confession.'

'Oh?'

174

'Oh, exactly. Mandy's first admission to hospital. She went of her own accord. Marsh withheld the heroin as he said he would. She was also afraid of what he might do to her. He turns up the next day, only to frighten her further, to bring her back into line. She discharges herself. The night he beat her up, it wasn't solely because she was keeping part of the money – she's also tried to do her own deal with the drugs.'

'You come across some charming people in your line of work, don't you? Could I have another glass of wine, please?'

'Sorry, love.' Ian looked at his own glass. He'd been talking so much it was still half full. He swallowed the contents in several large gulps and went up to the bar.

'Your round next time,' he said. 'You are a working woman, after all.'

'You were saying?' Moira rapidly changed the subject.

'Philpotts knows, probably through Danny, where the drugs are picked up. She tried to get there first. And that's where Charlie comes in again.'

'Sounds as if your Charlie would have made a good copper. He seems to have known what was going on everywhere.'

Ian was not sure whether this was meant as an insult to his own intelligence but decided to ignore it.

'The drop is made. Hardly thriller story stuff. The old tale, a council rubbish bin. Philpotts gets there, sees Marsh drop the money and waits. Some time later Danny Grant comes along, collects the money and leaves the drugs. They're always wrapped in rubbish, in packets hidden in bags of vegetable peelings or junk-food paper. Philpotts isn't quick enough. Marsh catches her. And meanwhile, our Charlie, who's been hanging around and who frequently goes through bins for bits of food or whatever else he thinks he can use, dips in his hand, comes up with a McDonald's container in which there's

175

some leftovers and takes it away. Imagine his surprise when he discovers what else is in there.'

'Does he know what it is?'

'We think he must have. He shoves it in his pocket anyway. However, he doesn't get far before Marsh goes tearing after him and retrieves the package.'

'So Marsh killed Charlie?'

'No. He shoves him around a bit but Charlie offers no resistance. It doesn't fit anyway. It would mean Marsh was already armed with a knife, a fairly large one, difficult to conceal, and the timing's all wrong. It was too early in the evening.'

'Have you picked up Danny Grant?'

'No. That's not up to us now. According to Marsh he's still at sea. Felixstowe'll get him. And I'm pretty certain we'll soon have Alex Chambers. Never uses an alias. It might take a while, but we'll have him. Now, I think it's time you took your pretty little self up to the bar and bought the old man a drink.'

'Half, is it?'

Ian slapped her playfully on the bottom. And then it struck him. Jokingly Moira had asked if he wanted a half. It was only a joke because she knew exactly his likes and dislikes, and she knew them because they'd been together a long time. Ian only drank pints.

So what did Charlie want with drugs? He wasn't a user. But perhaps he knew someone who was.

'I'm setting the alarm for six thirty,' he told Moira as they got ready for bed. 'There's no need for you to get up.'

'You know, don't you?' she said as she turned on her side and pulled his arm across her.

'I believe I do,' he replied and promptly fell asleep.

176

14

'Sir?'

'You heard me, Markham, I need a book listing the names and dates of authors. No, I don't know what it's called. Just find me one. Wait. I think my wife may have one.' Markham raised his eyes to the ceiling. He had no idea what was going on.

It was gone half-past two. Moira should be home. He prayed she hadn't chosen that afternoon to go shopping. He dialled his home number.

'What on earth do you want to know that for?'

'Just get it out, will you? I want you to look something up.' He gave her a name. 'Ring me back. Either way.'

As bemused as Markham she went to do his bidding. 'A please or thank you wouldn't come amiss,' she grumbled to herself as she opened the guide to English Literature.

Ian had spent the whole morning discovering there was no William Golding listed under any branch of medicine, not now and not for the period when he would have been working. None, that is, who was not still happily and legally practising or who was not retired. And no Golding had been struck off between the approximate dates they were working to. However, there were many medical practitioners with the initials W. G. and, as Ian well knew, when people decide to change their name they frequently stick to the same initials. In this case he thought it was deliberate.

He snatched up the receiver on his private line as soon as the phone rang.

'Ian? I've found it. It's here. Walter Greenwood. Born 1903. He wrote *Love on the Dole*. I didn't know that.'

'Did he now? Well, it doesn't matter what he wrote, only that he exists.'

'But surely he didn't . . .' but it was too late, Ian had already hung up. She would have to wait until this evening before he enlightened her.

'Oh, yes. Very clever,' Ian said to Barry and Markham, who were also waiting to be enlightened. 'Not only does he use the same initials, he picks another author's name.'

'I'm sorry if I appear unduly stupid, but what the hell are you talking about?'

'Can't you see it, Barry? Can't either of you see it yet?'

It appeared they couldn't. 'Will the pair of you stop bobbing around and sit down. Markham, the man you brought in, the vagrant, he told us his name was William Golding, and that's the name he's been going under since he was struck off. He even made a joke of it, about not being related to that author. All right,' he added, realising that Barry got the point but that it was lost on Markham, 'not everyone would know. William Golding. Ever heard of *Lord of the Flies*?'

'I thought it was a film.'

Ian sighed. Markham's literary education would have to wait for another time.

'Well, I'm betting our man Golding is really called Walter Greenwood. We've contacted every medical body there is. No William Golding. Not our man anyway. Dear God, Markham, can't you see it? By chance or design the man's parents gave him the name of an author. He wrote *Love on the Dole*, by the way.' Even Barry looked impressed. Ian did not bother to explain he

178

didn't know it himself until a few minutes ago. 'When he decided to change his name he used the same initials and another literary connection.'

'I thought he studied medicine.'

'He did, Markham, he did, but believe it or not there are actually people out there who read for pleasure. It seems to fit. I have here a list of the names of doctors struck off about fifteen years ago. There is a Walter Greenwood amongst them. We shall now find out if they are one and the same person. I think we'll find they are. Both of you get on to it. I want the full details surrounding his dismissal, and even back beyond that. Go back to his university days and his teaching hospital. Use as many men as you need. I want to know everything about that man.'

Markham and Barry got up to leave. As they opened the door DC Alan Campbell was on his way in.

'More good news, sir. Alex Chambers has been picked up.'

'Come in, Alan. You two go ahead.'

'Tell me,' Ian said when there were only two of them in the room.

'When he left here he didn't know we were on to him. Seems he realised he'd come to the end of the road with his cousin and he's the sort of man who can really only survive in cities. He was back at his old place in London. According to the Met his diary makes for fascinating reading. Although Chambers has no record some of the people he's in contact with are no strangers to Her Majesty's Prison Service.'

'So the Met'll owe us a few favours. Good. Go on.'

'He knows the score, does Chambers. Asked for his solicitor immediately. He knows if he spills the beans he'll get away lightly. He's no previous, no violence, never even been at the scene.'

'Still a villain, though, Alan, still a villain.'

179

'Yes, sir. He doesn't know where the JC Warehousing goods went. That's all he's saying at the moment. They haven't had time to find out more. They're sending him up with an escort tonight.'

'Good. The Super's going to be more than impressed with this lot.'

'What's going to happen about the Philpotts girl?'

'Not much, I shouldn't think. Apart from taking drugs we've got nothing on her. It might be for the best if she does go back with her parents.'

'Get her off our patch, you mean?'

'I'm afraid I do. Not the right attitude, I know, but you know the success rate. She'll be back on them as soon as someone's back is turned. Better there than here. Anyway, let's wait and see, shall we?'

Ian took himself down to the canteen for what he considered a deserved fry-up. He had to be right about this Golding/Greenwood thing. He just had to be.

'Well done, Judy.'

'It wasn't difficult, not once I told her we'd arrested Victor Marsh. Everything fits in with what we know so far. She admitted to the drugs and prostitution, she knew Danny's part in it and she also confirmed that Dixon and O'Doyle were not aware of her habit. She didn't know they knew now because they'd never mentioned it.'

'What's she going to do?'

'The parents are taking her home. She's promised to go to a rehab centre and all the rest of it. I don't envy them, they've got a long, hard struggle ahead. And from what I know of that girl she'll never make good.'

'We can but hope.' Ian was smiling. It seemed as if Mandy Philpotts would no longer be his problem.

'She also admits she was with Basil Wainright on the

Thursday night. The night he told Mrs Wainright he was still abroad. It was an all-night session. Marsh arranged it. He felt he was losing his grip on Wainright, that he might change his mind about letting them use his place. They booked into an hotel. It's on record that way. He'd got something to hold over his head.'

There was nothing Ian could do now but wait until he heard the outcome of Markham and Barry's inquiries.

As he sat at his desk smoking a relaxing cigarette he thought about Mr and Mrs Philpotts. He could see their side of it. No matter what they did, your kids were still your kids. He prayed he would never have to face that problem with Mark.

DC Winston Emmanuel had the dubious pleasure of interviewing Alex Chambers when at last he was brought by escort to Rickenham Green.

Chambers was almost philosophical about the whole thing. He knew it couldn't last for ever. He'd already had one or two narrow escapes. To ensure he was treated leniently he told them everything he knew. He named names and he gave addresses.

'And where are the goods?' Winston asked.

'The videos and camcorders? I really don't know. That's the way it worked. The less we knew about each part of the operation, the better. But if you want my educated guess, Glasgow.'

'What makes you say that?'

'Jimmy McKendrick was involved. He only deals in Glasgow.'

Winston made a note to contact Glasgow after the interview. 'So how come you still had one?'

'Insurance.'

'Explain?'

'In case my dear cousin got cold feet. It didn't work

out quite like I expected. I was going to have it delivered to his home. As a present. As an expression of my fondness for him and his wife, if he caused any trouble, that is. That night, in the Prince William, I got my landlady to bring it round. All wrapped up, it was, she wasn't involved. Didn't even know what she was bringing. Not bad, that one, she'd've done anything for me.'

The only thing Winston Emmanuel could say in Alex Chambers' favour was that he seemed genuinely sorry about his cousin's attempted suicide.

'Poor bastard,' he said. 'Nothing's worth that.'

'Go and get him,' the Chief said with grim satisfaction.

Walter Greenwood, also known as William Golding, made no protest when the two officers, backed up by a second car, walked towards him and told him he was under arrest. They read him his rights and escorted him across the waste ground. He made no attempt to run for it, no attempt to pull the murder weapon from beneath his coat where it had been all the time. He had been living on borrowed time for too many years.

'I thought you saw through me right away, Chief Inspector,' he said later. 'You disappointed me. Clever of you to spot the name, though, not many of your ilk would've done so.'

The Chief ignored the insult to the intelligence of his men.

'We now have documentary evidence of your medical career. Hardly one to be proud of.'

'I told you during our very first conversation the sort of man I am.'

'Not entirely. You missed out a couple of minor details. Such as the death of two of your patients.'

'Ah, yes, but that would've made it rather easy for you, wouldn't it. Besides, I thought you would have investigated my past immediately. I dropped enough hints.'

The Chief was struggling to keep his anger under control. The man was trying to make a fool of him. No wonder Markham had reacted the way he did when he first brought Greenwood in. He was facing total equanimity, complete cold-bloodedness, and there was nothing he could do about it. But he'd got what he wanted. A signed confession. And Charlie's killer.

'Chief Inspector,' Greenwood was saying, 'I have lived fifteen years with the knowledge that one day I was sure to be found. It hasn't been easy. In fact, over the years it became worse. Then along came Charlie. Once I knew that he knew, well, he had to go. It was as simple as that. At my time of life rough living isn't what it was. It might not be easy to conform to the confines of a prison cell but I can assure you a warm bed and regular meals begin to appeal. Now, there is nothing more I can add to my statement, and I'm sure you're ready to go home, so unless there's anything else you want to know?'

The Chief appraised the man opposite him. Not all, but some of the bravado was front, he guessed. Greenwood was tired and drawn but there was something different about him. The long wait was over.

'Ian, you look shattered. It's over, isn't it?'

Ian rubbed his temple between thumb and forefinger. The adrenalin which had kept him going no longer flowed. Despite his complaints of hardly any sleep he always got by, until a case was over. Then it hit him.

'Yes. It's over.'

'I'll run you a bath.' The time for talking would come later. The time when he would ask her why he hadn't seen it sooner, why he had missed vital clues. For now a bath and some food.

Ian lay, trying to relax. The water cooled and he added more hot. Gradually the tension seeped away. His mind wandered on to other subjects, the relationship between his son and Emma, and whether it would develop into something more. He had known Moira since she was seventeen. But he was already thirty-two by then. He must let Mark make his own choices, however hard they might be.

At last he began to appreciate that it really was over, that all that remained was some tidying up, and that tomorrow was Saturday and he would be free to go and watch Norwich.

'Look,' Moira said when she brought him a whisky to sip in the bath, 'why don't we make up that foursome with Barry and Lucy tomorrow?'

'Good idea. I won't be late but as it's Saturday it might be best to book somewhere. Why don't you ring Barry now?'

'I will. What do you mean, late? Oh, don't tell me. Football.'

He smiled. 'I'm afraid so. I'll have to go in for an hour in the morning, but I'll leave it until late and go straight from there. How does that suit you?'

'Fine. If they're free where shall I book?'

'That'll be up to Barry. He's paying.'

'It'll be a curry then. He's not renowned for splashing out on anything more.'

Barry was just on his way to pick up Lucy when Moira called. He said he was sure it was all right and to leave the arrangements to him.

Moira went back to the living-room to turn up the hem on the skirt of a new suit she'd bought.

'No need for you to've come in,' Ian said to Barry on Saturday morning.

'It's Lucy's Saturday at the bank and I've got nothing else to do. And I wanted to read Greenwood's statement.'

'Born with the proverbial spoon, wasn't he,' he commented later. 'Daddy paying for his education, a place in medical school, etc.'

'But he only just scraped through. You'll see when you read the other reports the type of man he was, or is. Right from the start he was put down as a bit slapdash, a bit of a dreamer, but he was young and inexperienced. He was given the benefit of the doubt. What wasn't known at the time was that he was already drinking heavily.'

'Yes. Able to do so with the allowance his father gave him on top of his salary.'

'Not much of a salary then.'

'Even so. The man obviously spoiled him. Then he gets into drugs. How do they do it? Nick it from the medicine trolley?'

'Come on, Barry, you ask around any city hospital. There's usually enough dope in the nurses' home to get high for a month.'

'So he qualified, completed his first year as a hospital doctor but wasn't given a permanent post. He got a reference though.'

'But he wasn't so lucky the second time. He started making mistakes. It was suggested he might be better off elsewhere. By dint of his charm and personality, he landed another post. His reference was one of those non-committal ones.'

'Closed shop? All medics sticking together?'

'Possibly, but the man who gave us this information said they still believed he would make a good doctor, that he was a natural with patients and that the rough edges could be smoothed away.'

'But they didn't fancy the wood shavings on their own floor.'

'It was the third job where the trouble really started. He did all right for nearly a year, no visible signs of his drinking, but he'd learned to hide it by then, and his tolerance was at its highest. I spoke to his direct employer yesterday. Private medicine. He'd left the NHS by then. The man said there were a few discrepancies, medication prescribed in the wrong dosage, and he was given a warning. Things improved for a short time. He began to look ill and he was going through his money at a fast rate. Later it was discovered he'd been borrowing from his colleagues and not paying them back.'

'To finance the drugs?'

The Chief nodded as he lit a cigarette. 'Perhaps I should think about giving this up again.'

'No, please. I don't want to go through that again.' The Chief was hard to live with during his periods of abstinence.

'Then Greenwood disappeared. He knew he was in above his head. One patient had died. At first it didn't seem suspicious. The woman was seriously ill, possibly expected to die. Greenwood was called out during the night and administered her medication. It was only later, when a sister queried it, that it turned out to be an overdose.'

'Surely the post-mortem would've shown that?'

'No. One wasn't necessary. If a person's already being treated for an illness, whether they're at home or in hospital, and they die from what they've been diagnosed as having, no PM is necessary. However, the second occasion was a blatant mistake. Without going into technicalities, you can read the report yourself, a young man, in for a routine op, also died. This time there had to be an investigation. This was when Greenwood disappeared. It was another case of an overdose, this time a massive one. He'd prescribed a hundred instead of ten units of whatever the man was on.'

186

'And you wonder why I don't like hospitals. Jesus. It's frightening. Give us a fag, will you, Ian? All this talk's getting to me.'

'Greenwood was struck off in his absence. A letter was sent to his father's address once they realised he wasn't coming back. It's doubtful he ever received it. He never went back there.'

'And the police?'

'Called in too late. Greenwood was on a long week-end. Officially that is, so they didn't realise he was gone for four days. By then he'd hidden his tracks. They contacted his father but he didn't know where he was.'

'Didn't know or wasn't saying.'

'Didn't know. By that time he'd washed his hands of his son.'

'I can't remember reading about the case.'

'It was fifteen-odd years ago. You were still in school.'

'I can see why he scarpered, but why end up here?'

'He lived off his wits for several weeks, stealing food as and where he could. He became ill, the drugs, or by then lack of them, didn't help, and undernourished. He was so ill he had no option but to get help. He used everyone he could think of, and he'd know, through his training, which organisations would guarantee confidentiality. The Salvation Army, Samaritans, you name it. And he also knew that no one would be looking for the ill, dirty vagrant he'd become. Even the police were working on the theory he'd probably left the country.'

'Still doesn't explain what he's doing here.'

'He says he not only found that he could exist, but he became used to the life. Enjoyed it almost. He moved from place to place and eventually the fuss died down. However, the case is still open and according to his last hospital, the parents of the young man who died have never given up hope of finding Greenwood.'

'How could he live with himself? All those years, knowing what he'd done because of his own self-indulgence. So are you saying it was pure chance that he landed on us?'

'No. He was born and bred in Suffolk. Some homing instinct, maybe. Who knows? He was thinking it was time to move on when he came across Charlie.'

'He knew him?'

'No. It was the other way around. Charlie recognised him. You see, at one time Charlie worked for Greenwood's father.'

'No.'

'Absolutely true. Think about it. Charlie apparently never held down a job for long. He took casual labour as and when he found it. But he was happy for a while with Greenwood senior, until he got itchy feet again. Now Charlie would notice the family in the big house far more than they would him, especially one such as Greenwood. We spoke to Greenwood senior. He's in his eighties but he's all there. He confirmed this.'

'It must've been a shock, his son turning up after fifteen years.'

'If it was, he didn't show it. One of the old school. Well-mannered and unflappable. He lives just outside Bury St Edmunds. Come on, all this talking's giving me a thirst. Fancy a pint?'

They strolled up to the Feathers, enjoying a milder morning. The streets were busy. Shoppers hurried past laden with carrier bags and groups of teenagers loitered in shop doorways. The traffic was at a standstill while someone waited for a car to pull out so that they could take the parking space. Diesel fumes mingled with the smell of frying fish and chips. The quietness of the pub was welcome after the noise and bustle.

The landlord was sitting on the customer side of the bar reading one of the brewery publications and enjoying his own cigarette before things got busy. He placed it in an ashtray and went behind.

'A pint of lager and a bitter,' Barry said.

'No, I'll have a bottled Guinness for a change. No need to look like that. I'm driving this afternoon.'

'Ah, yes. The Canaries.'

They looked round for a suitable table. Three ancient men sat in one corner, all wearing caps. A whippet sat at the feet of one of the men. The only other customer was a solitary woman, shopping on the chair beside her as she sipped what looked like a glass of port.

'So Charlie recognises Greenwood.'

'Yes. And he made the mistake of telling him so. He'd been getting the money from Christopher Chambers, you see, and for once in their lives the tables were turned. Charlie was now top dog. He was the one with funds. He told Greenwood, perhaps he boasted about it, then the following week he gets twenty. It must've been hard to keep quiet about it. However, he wants to be friends with the man, they did, after all, know each other years ago. When he finds the drugs, that's when he tells Greenwood he knows who he is. He says he's going to give them to him. Greenwood's enraged. Not only does Charlie know who he is, and has done so ever since they came together, he knows about his past life. Worse is that Greenwood was so near to getting his hands on the drugs but Charlie's messed it up.'

'So he stabs him.'

'He's killed twice before. Not deliberately, but he has killed. And he's getting to the end of his tether. Maybe he was hoping we'd catch him. The life he's got to look forward to now will be better than the one he's used to.'

'What bugs me,' Ian said after he refused a second drink and they were ready to leave, 'is that he had the murder weapon on him all the time. The one place we never thought of looking.'

189

'Well, you've got him now. Come on, if we're going, let's go. And, please, I beg of you. Spare me and Lucy the details of the match when we see you tonight.'

'I'll try,' Ian said, smiling, 'but I can't promise.'

The meal was a great success. Lucy and Moira hit it off from the start. When they'd finished eating, Moira excused herself and went upstairs to the ladies. When she returned Ian stood up and slid the table out to allow her to return to her seat easily.

'Is that new?' he asked.

'My suit? Yes. Do you like it?'

'It's very smart.'

'It took you long enough to notice. I thought you were supposed to be observant.'

'Oh, I am. It's just that I was too busy looking at the legs.'

'Oh, honestly, Ian.' But she was pleased at the compliment.

'Who wants coffee?' Barry asked, embarrassed by his boss's behaviour. 'And a brandy? To celebrate the end of the case.' They all agreed.

'What's the matter, Ian?' Moira asked, seeing his face fall. 'I thought it was all tied up.'

'Oh, it is. It's just so infuriating. An open goal in the last minute of the game and they manage to miss it.'

'There's always next week,' Barry interrupted quickly. 'Now, why don't we let Lucy tell us all about investment trusts? It's got to be more interesting than football.'

'Very well, point taken. But couldn't I just . . .?'

'No,' Ian's three companions said in unison.

'You can tell me later. When I'm asleep,' Moira added.

Ian had to give in. He knew when he was beaten. And he had the consolation of guessing if his wife had purchased new underwear to go with the suit.

190